SAVE OUR CHILDREN SAVE OUR SCHOOL
PEARSON BROKE THE GOLDEN RULE

SAVE OUR CHILDREN SAVE OUR SCHOOL PEARSON BROKE THE GOLDEN RULE

DENNY TAYLOR

NEW YORK, NY

GARN PRESS

NEW YORK, NY

Published by Garn Press, LLC
New York, NY
www.garnpress.com

Book and cover design by Ben James Taylor/Garn Press
Cover art by Malia Hughes, "Mother Earth", Oil Painting

Publisher's Cataloging-in-Publication Data
Taylor, Denny, 1947-
Save our children, save our school, Pearson broke the golden rule / Denny Taylor.
    pages cm
    Includes bibliographical references.
    ISBN: 978-0-9899106-4-4 (pbk.)
    ISBN: 978-0-9899106-5-1 (e-book)
1. Parody. 2. Political satire. 3. Imaginary conversations. 4. Education—Anecdotes, facetiae, satire, etc. 5. Democracy and education. 6. Education and state.   I. Title.
    PN6231.P6 .T39 2014
    320.0207—dc23
                        2013952785

In Defense of Children

And for

Parents and Teachers

Against

Tyranny

For

Maya Angelou

Hannah Arendt

Emilia Ferriero

Maxine Greene

Yetta Goodman

Wangari Maathai

Toni Morrison

Adrienne Rich

Louise Rosenblatt

Mina Shaughnessy

Simone Weil

Virginia Woolf

And

Noam Chomsky

These venerable scholars frame my scholarship and everyday
existence

I am deeply grateful

It is not conceivable that our culture will forget that it needs children. But it is halfway toward forgetting that children need childhood. Those who insist on remembering shall perform a noble service.

Neil Postman, 1982

The Disappearance of Childhood[1]

If, as is our custom, the teachers undertake to regulate many minds of such different capacities and forms with the same lesson and a similar measure of guidance, it is no wonder if in the whole race of children they find barely two or three who reap any proper fruit from their teaching.

Michel de Montaigne, 1579

The Complete Essays of Montaigne[2]

CONTENTS

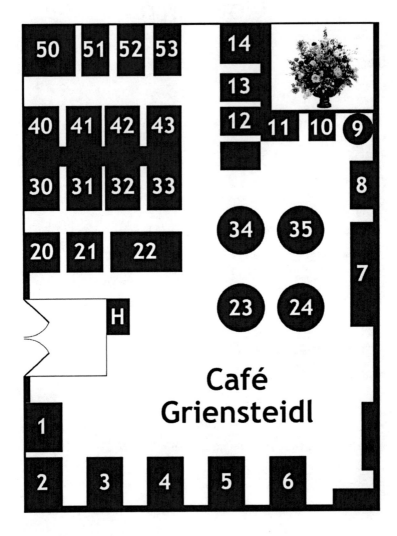

The imaginary conversations in Acts Two, Three and Four take place in Café Griensteidl. The seating plan of the Café provides the reader with the locations of the diners who participate in the satire.

AUTHOR'S NOTE

This book is a work of dissent. It is a satirical challenge to the political and corporate establishment that is systematically dismantling the public education system in the United States.

In "More Pain, Better Sentences", in the *London Review of Books*,[3] Adam Mars-Jones, writes," Satirists diagnose rather than prescribe: they clear weeds with a flamethrower but offer no suggestions about planting." Contrarian in every aspect, this satire includes suggestions for flowers to replace the choking weeds.

In a conversation with a lawyer about the satire I mentioned that the work begins at the end with an imaginary conversation with Mother Earth.

"That's okay," she said. "Mother Earth has no rights."

"Mother Earth has every right," I wanted to say, but didn't.

Mother Earth and our children have every right and we must do what we can to protect them. And so, a satirical work that defies any other categorization.

The title is a parody on a nursery rhyme. I have used *golden rule* in the historical sense of the *ethic of reciprocity* that travels easily in and between cultures and religions requiring empathy, mutual support, and solidarity in our commitment to each other and to the common good.

The golden rule is also term used in economics to refer to equality of capital/income ratios, which is an abstract idea pontificated upon that actually as significance for future scenarios of climate change and ecological degradation. Whichever way we chose to use the golden rule the rights of people, especially children are being violated. Hence the line in the nursery rhyme relating to Pearson, which becomes the signifier of the breaking of the golden rule of caring for our common humanity.

1

The text splits genres and tears-up academic convention while remaining true to the imperative of scholarly referencing of works used. At Garn we have gone back and forth about superscripts in the text – should we include them in a book that is both fiction and non-fiction, art as well as science?

The book is going into production so a decision has to be made. Thus you will find superscripts in the text and the references at the back of the book, meticulously checked, organized for your use. Some poetic license has been taken in creating imaginary interactions between participants in this performance piece, but the statements made by the nine very rich men and the twelve venerable women scholars are verbatim. Similarly, quotes from other renowned participants in the conversation are verbatim and included in the reference list. The statements by the other diners at the fictitious Café Greindsteidl are derived from real statements made by parents and teachers who are resisting the Whole System Global Education Revolution which is being waged against them and their children.

A final note: I have been fortunate as an adult to be included in the imaginative games of many children. The book owes much to the children who have included me in their imaginative play, to doctoral students who have been ready to challenge the dominant discourse and explore imaginative ways of thinking, and to teachers who encourage their students to participate in projects and activities that are imaginative and creative as well as intellectually challenging. Without these experiences there would be no book.

Similarly, without David Taylor and Benjamin Taylor there would be no book or Garn Press. They are Garners par excellence. I am deeply grateful. I share with them any kind words about this satirical work, but claim the right to all errors that might exist.

Denny Taylor
New York, NY
July, 2014

*In which drama, comedy, and tragedy are combined to create
a cosmological allegory that focuses on scientific realism and
political skullduggery, to expose a global coup d'état that
threatens the present and future lives of our children*

THE END

"Done!" I say. "Just wrote the last sentence."

"What d'you think?" you say, gasping for breath. "Can they tag it?"

"Honestly?" I say. "I don't know?"

Your lungs are rasping and for a moment you cannot talk.

"It's possible," I say. "But I don't think so." I'm not sure if you can hear me. "

"The education of the world's children cannot be controlled by nine very rich misguided men," you say, weakened by the effort to speak, "who have neither taught nor been elected."

I wait, knowing there is more you want to say when you catch your breath.

"The masters of mankind!" you say. "They have never studied how humans learn. They know *nothing* –"

"*Nothing!*" you spit out the word.

"*Nothing* about human development. *Nothing* about how children learn language. *Nothing* about how they *use* language. Nothing about the brilliant imaginings of young children, *when they are given the opportunity*, to participate in great projects, both literary and scientific."

"They know *nothing*," you say, in a rasping whisper, "about how, when children are five or six, they learn about death"

"Rest," I say.

"I'm dying," you say. "Why rest?"

There are no words that I can speak or write upon the page.

"Such foppery," you say, with the irritation of an old woman at famous men who are her sons.

Catching your breath, your anger carries you through the next sentence.

"None of them have degrees in physics or biology so how can they dictate how children are taught science?"

"Most of them studied history," I say.

"And all they learned," you say, exasperated, "is that history repeats," another breath, "and they are the ones repeating it!"

"Witless fools!" you say, as you try to get comfortable. Your skin is wrinkled, parched and cracked, and your veins stand out, spread wide, like deltas of rivers choked with detritus. Every turn is a challenge.

"Did the oligarch really say they won't know for a decade if the experiment has worked?"

I nod.

"Arrogance!" you cry. "He has abandoned reason for madness."

"The objective is to make the outcomes of the revolution irreversible so there's no going back," I say.

"Fools!" you spit the word. "There *is* no going back."

"But we can change direction," I say.

Your eyes glitter with old tears, but are sharply focused.

"The two questions?" you ask.

"I answered them," I say, "but not in a way that would get me a high mark on a school assignment."

"Can they tag them?'

"Difficult," I say, smiling.

"Is it still the first chapter of *Keys to the Future*?"[4]

I shake my head.

"*Another book?*"

"'fraid so," I say.

"What kind of book?" you ask, urgently, not rasping as much.

"Not sure how you would categorize it," I say.

"Tell me!" you say, oozing droplets of topaz colored sweat.[5] [6]

"It was going to be a couple of paragraphs at the beginning of the first chapter of *Keys to the Future*, then a new first chapter, and then about thirty pages in I knew it was going to be a book."

"You write books like women have babies!" you say, spreading your arms wide before collapsing with a shudder.

"It's a problem," I say, laughing. "My books have books before I publish them."

"Non-fiction?"

"Non-fiction *and* fiction."

"Genres?"

"Multiple."

"Tell me!"

"Combines drama, comedy, and tragedy," I say. "It's a cosmological allegory that focuses on scientific realism and political skullduggery."

"Poetry?"

"I've included a young poet and the Bard."

"Which play?"

"Macbeth."[7]

"You'd better turn three times and spit," you say. "What about discourse?"

"Every form of utterance that seemed to fit," I say, on my second rotation. "Colloquial and formal speech, narrative and academic texts."

"Muddled?"

"Of course," I say, spitting. "What else could it be?"

"Swear."

"Hell and damnation!"

"That should do it!" you say, amused at my vehemence. "Tell me about the cover."

"You're on it," I say, wanting to reach out and hold your hand, but knowing I cannot.

"Not like this?" you say, looking down at the peaks and valleys of wreckage you have become.

"It's that beautiful painting of you when you were young," I say.

"I'm holding a bunch of flowers?"

"That's the one."

"And that fan!" you say, with anguish. "It's what I've become." You let out a sharp cry, a lament, and we are both lost in sorrow.

"The women?" you say.

"The twelve great scholars we talked about," I say, nodding.

"*Teachers,*" you say. "Great teachers."

We are both quiet. Time is passing. We both feel it.

"The book!" you say, suddenly, becoming agitated. "Who's going to read it?"

"Not sure," I say. "I really don't know."

"Let's hope they do," you say, the moment of excitement past, and the future looming. "And *act* fast before it's too late."

"Is this the end?" I ask mechanically, with no idea what I mean.

"Or the beginning," she says, without moving her lips.

"What do you mean?" I ask. "It's the beginning of the end, or something else is beginning?"[8]

In which the decision is made that the education of the world's children cannot be controlled by nine very rich and foolishly misguided men who have neither taught nor been elected.

ACT ONE

Let's begin, you and I, with an imaginary conversation about what it would take to make the Earth a child safe zone. And just like we did when we were children and had adventures playing imaginary games, let's start by framing the story.

"Dystopic," you say. "What else could it be in the time in which we live?"

"Children are tributes?" I say. "But the story is not based on the *Hunger Games.*"[9]

"Got it," you say.

"There are at least ten Voldemorts" I say.

"Ahh, *Harry Potter*," you say. "I always thought it was interesting that the maniacal obsession of the evil wizard in Rowling's novels was a student at Hogwarts School."[10]

"He wanted to destroy Harry, but he also wanted the school," I say. "Change what happens in schools and you change the future."

"Okay, we're on the same page," you say again, adding, "I'll play, but as you're writing you can set it up."

"Thanks," I say. "I think we just did. I hope it works. The book's written, but I'm back at the beginning, and I'm not sure –"

"This'll work," you say. "There's too much at stake for it not too."

"Okay," I say. "There are no wizards, but children are in great peril."

"Villains?"

"Very rich and powerful men with enormous egos," I say.

"Some wicked, some not, all of whom are foolishly misguided into thinking if they take control of the ways in which children are educated," you say, "they'll hold the keys to the future."

"Incalculable riches and enormous power –"

"That's good," I say. "They bamboozle the public with multi-million dollar ad campaigns about public schools failing, and how by changing the curriculum they can make the US more globally competitive."

"And close the gap between rich and poor."

"That too," I say, "while in reality the gap gets wider."

"What you're proposing in this imaginary conversation," you say, "is a linguistic coup."

"A coup d'état," I say, nodding, glad that you were once one of my doctoral students.

"A perverse *Willie Wonka* story?"[11] you say. "Kids being tested for chocolate?"

"A ticket to college, a job in the future," I say. "Offering an end to poverty and making the American people more prosperous."

"Only, what's really happening is the reverse," you say. "It's a propaganda nightmare. I was going to retire. Many principals that I know have left, but I'm hanging on for the sake of my teachers. They're being battered by the State. So are the kids. It's a totally abusive situation."

"A hostile insurgence," I say. "A well-financed private militia now occupies the language and thinking of children in US K-12 public schools."

"This isn't make-believe," you say. "This might be an imaginary conversation and we might be playing, but my take on it is that we are actually *being played*."

"Except we're excluded from the real conversation that's taking place," I say. "No one's listening to us. Teachers are being threatened into silence. They're being bullied. Many are afraid. Some are fighting back, but many are leaving the profession."

"Parents are excluded too," you say. "Some of them are much braver than us. In some ways the stakes are higher for them. Mothers see their children's suffering."

"They're fighting as if their children's lives are threatened," I say. "Intuitively many must know that the ways in which they are taught in school will determine the future of human life on Earth."

"The challenge is to expose how children and teachers in K-12 public schools have become a big data set for commercial gain," you say.

"To show in harsh light the linguistic aggression of the private sector," I say, nodding, "and how well-orchestrated systems of surveillance and interrogation have been put into place."

"And how do you propose to do that?" you ask, "without being tagged?"

"Tagged? You mean Knewton?" I ask.

"One hundred and eighty thousand students right now," Jose Ferreira, the CEO of Knewton says, entering the conversation.[12]

"He was a derivatives trader for Goldman Sachs," you say, "and a partner at Venture Capital, Draper Atlantic."

"By December it'll be 650,000," Ferreira says, "early next year it'll be in the millions and the next year it'll be closer to 10 million, and that's just through Knewton's partnership with Pearson.'"

"Oh, that's good," you say. "In an imaginary conversation the players can be played."

"Ferreira has said in a few years they'll have 100 million children tagged," I say. "I watched the video. He says, 'We literally know everything about what you know.'"

"Ferreira believes that 'everything in education is correlated to everything else,'" you say, quoting Ferreira, "'and that every single concept is correlated in a predictable way to everything else using psychometrics', right?"

"He has a derivatives trader's understanding of knowledge," I say. "Not a clue about systemic complexity in either the physical or social sciences."

"Dangerously naïve."

"He believes that if you produce data points at what he calls the 'granular level', you produce lots and lots of data," I say, nodding. "Every concept, every sentence gets tagged, cascading connections, observed patterns, significance calculated."

"Very scientific," you say. "Only it's not."

"Children are vassals, fill-in-the-blanks, only the blanks are not bubbles on some multiple-choice test," I say. "They are actually children whose minds are being manipulated."

You look troubled, but do not speak.

"Okay?"

"I'm thinking of the children in my school," you say. "It's overwhelming."

"It *is* overwhelming," I say. "Ferreira believes that if you can get all that tagging right you can tell the child she does better work when she has scrambled eggs for breakfast."

"So tell me again," you say, "What's the point of this imaginary conversation?"

"To create a text that can't be tagged."

"And why would we want to do that?"

"As an act of defiance," I say. "To support the resistance movement against the coup d'état, and to protest the destruction of K-12 *public* schools."

"Okay," you say, looking skeptical. "To resist the coup d'état that is bringing about the linguistic destruction of the K-12 public school system, you want to hit them with an imaginary text that they can't destroy."

"That's about it," I say. "Our only hope is to undermine the thinking on which the coup is based, because all the scientific evidence indicates there is much more than K-12 public education that depends upon it. Our children are in peril and we must act."

"Is that what you have written about in *Keys to the Future*?"

"Yes," I say. "That text is more formal. It's about the conditions, strategies, planning, and execution of the coup."

"D'you remember that doctoral seminar on Mikhail Bakhtin?"[13] you ask. "You began by asking if any of us had imaginary friends when we were children, and nearly all of us put our hands up?"

"Imaginary friends can be the key to creative thought," I say, nodding, "My imaginary friends are the scientists, philosophers, scholars, novelists and poets who live in the pages of books I read. *The Life of the Mind*,[14] Hannah Arendt calls it, and Maxine Green writes about it in *Releasing the Imagination* –"[15]

"That's what this struggle is all about isn't it," you say. "The right of children to have that experience. To live in their imaginations, connect to the world, sensory and non-sensory, to live their lives in thoughtful ways, empathetic and rational, and not be re-programmed by some rich and powerful men for the perverse misguided purpose of establishing a global educational orthodoxy."

"Children have the right to connect to the world and live their lives in thoughtful ways," I say, "combining emotion and reason. Language is what makes us human. It's public. Part of the commons. The private sector can't own it, not without violating children's human rights *and* civil rights."

"Daniel Ferguson wrote about that," you say, "in *Rethinking Schools*[16] in his response to David Coleman's video[17] of himself and how Coleman would teach a "close reading" of Martin Luther King Jr.'s 1963 *Letter from Birmingham Jail.*"[18]

"Ferguson responded by doing "a close reading" of Coleman's video," I say, "and clearly demonstrates that Coleman's "lesson" misses the deep meaning of the letter."

"Coleman's agenda," Ferguson points out, joining the conversation, "most resembles King's description of 'the white moderate .... more devoted to order than justice.' King did 'set an agenda,' and the agenda is racial equality and social justice, not a model for test-friendly reading instruction."

"There is a grand irony in the last few minutes of the video," Ferguson says, "when Coleman praises King for not just responding to what was in the clergyman's letter, 'but pointing out how critical is what's not in the letter.' Why then, is it problematic to let students do the same, to let their world inform their reading?"

"Critical literacy argues that students' sense of their own realities should never be treated as outside the meaning of a text," Ferguson continues, his words echoing through the text of our imaginary conversation. "To do so is to infringe on their rights to literacy. In other words, literacy is a civil and human right; having your own experiences, knowledge, opinions valued is a right as well. Despite praise for King's rhetoric, Coleman promotes a system that creates outsiders of students in their own classrooms."

"The only problem, forgive me for saying this so bluntly," Coleman says, joining the conversation "as you grow up in this world you realize people really don't give a shit about want you feel or what you think."[19] His language in the video is explicit, but is cleaned up in the NYSED transcript.[20]

"Chalk one up to Ferguson," you say. "He has the teaching experience and scientific research, all Coleman has is unsupported opinion."

"And Ferguson grew up in Birmingham," I say, "Coleman trivialized

King's letter, reduced it to a lesson *on* the Common Core. Coleman crossed a line and Ferguson called him on it."

"Okay," I say. "Let's blur the boundaries between what we think and what we feel, combine reason with emotion, rational thought and empathy, write factual information in a fictional form, cross over between the physical and social sciences, and stretch what can be said in a particular context, at a particular time, and in a particular way."

"Challenging," you say. "Resisting the coup d'état that's taking place by playing a grown-up version of a child's game of make-believe."

"The coup d'état is an assault on children's language and thinking," I say, "our only hope is to use all the linguistic resources at our disposal to close the book on the coup."

"Poetic justice," you say, with a smile. "Did you see the letter Maya Angelou and 120 authors and illustrators of books for children wrote to President Obama?"[21]

"We the undersigned," May Angelou says, joining us to read the letter, "write to express our concern for our readers, their parents and teachers. We are alarmed at the negative impact of excessive school testing mandates, including your Administration's own initiatives, on children's love of reading and literature."

"Our public school students spend far too much time preparing for reading tests and too little time curling up with books that fire their imaginations," Maya Angelou continues.

"It's not about testing and reading schemes, but about loving stories and passing on that passion to our children," Michael Morpurgo, the author of the Tony Award Winner *War Horse*,[22] says.

"We are creating a generation that hates reading and feels noting but hostility for literature," Philip Pullman, the author of *The Golden Compass*[23] says.

"This year has seen a growing national wave of protest against testing overuse and abuse," Maya Angelou concludes, speaking as she always does with majestic grace. "As the authors and illustrators of books for children, we feel a special responsibility to advocate for change. We offer our full support for a national campaign to change the way we assess learning so that schools nurture creativity, exploration, and a love of literature from the first day of school through high school graduation."

"*Phenomenal Woman!*"[24] you cry as she leaves the page, and I notice there are tears in your eyes.

"Not all writing can be tagged," I say again, smiling. "It's the reason for the Coleman Common Core shift to non-fiction. Fiction creates problems for multiple comparisons, which is the essence of big data. The purpose of our imaginary conservation is to bend genres, and give a practical demonstration of how language and thinking are not synonymous with text complexity. The text we're about to create will be a linguistic feat – a scientific report, a philosophical tract, a historic account, a novel, or a play – that can't be tagged."

"The point is fiction and non-fiction are not always separate categories," I continue. "When children play imaginary games they participate in language games that are grounded in their direct experiences of their everyday lives. This sharing of their dreams, hopes, and fears is critical to their emerging humanity –"

"Go on," you say.

"Rigor, empathy and imagination become the signature of their writing in a similar way to when great writers write," I rush on. "If this were not the case, and if non-fiction and fiction were indeed separate categories, we would never have felt the pleasure or felt the pain of reading, "*I Know Why the Cage Bird Sings*,[25] or *War Horse*, or *The Golden Compass*, or experience the way Martin Luther King Jr. moved the nation with *I Have a Dream*."[26] [27]

"I was thinking about Coleman," you say. "Denying the experiences of others is egotistical and selfish. He comes across as spoilt, as if he is used to getting his own way."

"If you like," I say, "in this act of transgression, as we protest the coup d'état, we can make this imaginary conversation a school assignment."

"Why not? Our task?"

"To use every literary device at our disposal," I say, "to make the case that there are two threats to our children that impact every aspect of their present and future lives," I say.

"This is more than an exercise," you say. "I can almost feel that my role is about to change. Can I come back?" you ask. "I like the imaginary role I am playing."

"Of course," I say. "You know it's more than an imaginary role that you're playing."

And so it begins. An imaginary conversation is about to take place that is nested in another imaginary conversation.

Enough said. The scene shifts to Café Griensteidl.

ACT TWO

We are two women having lunch. For the men who are reading it is good to stretch. Women so often have to switch their gender to communicate in a public arena.

Let's pretend we are meeting at a bistro, Café Griensteidl in Manhattan. The food is good and it is always busy. It is close to Lincoln Center and usually filled with people from the arts, writers, actors, opera singers, musicians, and it often seems that the conversations overheard are so fantastical they seem made up.

I arrive early and sit at table 35 with a good vantage point to view the scene.

Rupert Murdoch and Joel Klein are sitting opposite each other in the far corner at table 9, with a huge green pottery urn of spring flowers behind them. No one is sitting at tables 8 and 10. Sir Michael Barber is sitting next to Klein with his back to the room but facing the huge mirror, which gives him an expansive view and we, in the mirror, can see him too.

You arrive a little late. You look around searching the tables, and as I wave you spread your arms wide and give a little shrug.

"Traffic!" you say. "And no taxis when you want one! You'd think the UN General Assembly is in here by the security outside."

The greeting is elaborate. Both cheeks. I ask about your flight. You talk about the freezing temperatures in New York. "It's colder than Stockholm," you say. We talk about family, the death of my mother, the medical condition of your mother, her resiliency, her long life, and her fragility now she is very old.

The game is on.

I am living in New York. Retired. Emerita. I've started a small publishing company, but I am continuing my research and writing. Your career is far more illustrious. You are in New York for a meeting of *Future Earth*[28] at the United Nations. You've been on leave from your university in Copenhagen, and you have been participating in a research project at the Stockholm Resiliency Center. You spend a considerable amount of time in Sweden, but you home is in Denmark, which is where you were born and grew up. We met at the *Planet Under Pressure* conference[29] in London in 2012, and we have corresponded about the research we are both doing on the relationships between people and the planet.

We talk briefly about your research on the biophysical aspects of planetary boundaries, and how critical social equity is to global sustainability. My own research on enhancing human well-being at a time when the planet is rapidly changing intersects with your research on achieving an equitable operating space for humanity. We have had previous conversations about the many ways in which greater   equality, especially in income, has shown to be directly related to an increase in life expectancy, a decrease in homicide rates, a drop in rates of mental illness, and a very significant improvement in education outcomes.

Inevitably the UN Intergovernmental Panel on Climate Change report *Summary for Policy Makers* on *Impacts, Adaptation and Vulnerabilities*,[30] which has just been published, is a topic of conversation. You participated in the construction of the report and I have read it. We have both read the reports in the *The Guardian* and *The New York Times*. The evidence is overwhelming that the impacts of climate change are likely to be severe, pervasive and irreversible.

"The report doesn't state anything that we don't already know," you say. "But the data are now irrefutable that the drivers of climate-related hazards and the vulnerability of human and natural systems are due to socioeconomic processes."

You talk about social-ecological traps[31] and of the heightened vulnerabilities to human life on Earth occurring as a product of intersecting social processes that result in inequalities in socioeconomic status and income. You say, quoting the IPCC report, "Such social processes include, for example, discrimination on the basis of gender, class, ethnicity, age and (dis)ability."

"We seem to have totally forgotten," I say, "that human and natural systems are interlinked, and that the anthropogenic changes are going to be severe."

Human stressors on Earth systems plus adaptation and mitigation are our usual topics of conversation, and so today when we have lunch that is the discussion we both expect to take place, and in a way it does, but perhaps not in a way either of us anticipates.

"What are you writing?" you ask.

"It's about the richest man on Earth taking over the most powerful country in the world in a coup d'état."

"A novel!" you exclaim. "Dystopic, of course, how could it be otherwise."

"Dystopic, yes," I reply, with a smile, "but not a novel."

You look surprised. Raise an eyebrow. It is not the response you expected.

"The richest man on Earth? Carlos Slim?" you ask, floundering. There is no context for this conversation except of course it is actually as much about what is happening to the planet as it is about what is happening to our children.

"Bill Gates," I say, and then deadpan, "It's also about a media mogul who takes control of the free press, newspapers, television."

"Rupert Murdoch?" You frown and look up at the ceiling before looking sharp eyed straight at me. "Murdoch I get, but Gates? He's given so much."

"So it would seem," I say.

"What I'm doing is examining the conditions, strategies, planning, and execution of the not-so-sudden illegal seizure of the United States most precious possession."

"Xbox One?" you ask.. "Microsoft's new videogame is called Titanfall."

You are laughing, and I can't help myself, I laugh too, but you realize I am serious. "Come on, tell me," you say. "What *is* the United States most precious possession?"

"It's children," I say. "The nation's children."

Neither of us speaks for a moment. We have both worked in places where children have experienced mass trauma, witnessed what can happen when there is a natural disaster, or worse, a human disaster in which there is unspeakable violence and regions of armed conflict, remembering the children who haunt us because of the desperate circumstances in which they struggled to survive. For many of us who live in this space, tears of despair are so often accompanied with laughter, and it can become habitual as if self-administering a shot of endorphins to increase hope and diminish pain.

The restaurant is noisy, filled with animated conversations, and creative energy emanating both from the kitchen and from the crowded tables. We focus on the menu. The waiter comes over and the memories that so frequently occupy our minds return to their resting place, and we are both extravagant in our choices of dishes in this imaginary meal. We listen to the specials for today and order French onion soup, and pick from a list of appetizers, shaved Brussels sprouts with pear and cider vinaigrette, fried baby artichokes with shishito peppers, grilled lemon, and bagna cauda aioli –"

"And *frites!*" I say.

"And the roasted button mushrooms," you say, looking up at the waiter with a smile.

"Tap or bottled water?" he asks.

"Tap," we both say.

"This is a follow-up to *Nineteen Clues*?"[32] It sounds like a question, but it's actually a statement. "How could you do otherwise? *Clues* makes it difficult to shut the book on the issues your raise, but –," you look troubled, "it's difficult to imagine Gates as the most phenomenal evil genius the world has ever known. Do you remember the movie *Goldfinger*?"[33]

We can't help ourselves, we both laugh.

"I don't think I would characterize him that way," I say, "but he's well on the way to pulling off the most daring heist in the history of the USA."

"It's absurd, too abstract." you say. "Okay. You're a scientist. I suppose we can approach this another way, as an argument about what constitutes scientific knowledge. We're both convinced there is an urgent need to ditch narrow definitions of *the* scientific method," you say, smiling, "as if there is only one way of doing science."

"Systemic complexity!" Now I am smiling. "Makes for a more interesting conversation than one about conspiracy theories!"

"So tell me what do you mean by conditions? Strategies? Planning? Execution? I need data, analysis, it's all too –," she searches for words, "how do you say it? Too phantasmagorical?"

By framing the conversation as a discussion about science you place our feet firmly on familiar ground.

"When I wrote *Nineteen Clues*," I say, "I didn't have much of an inkling about Gates. Remember, I began the research for that book in 2009, and the book documents events in 2012 using hindsight to verify the interpretations of the documentation about the events that were taking place. Much has happened since then that should be cause for very serious concern, not only here in the US, but in other countries around the world."

"Go on."

"You know all my research begins with the same question," I begin. "What would it take to make the Earth a child safe zone?"

"I'm uncomfortable with such grand questions," you say, "but in some ways it *is* the question we're all asking."

"I consider there to be two major threats."

"Only two?"

"With sub-parts," I say, and again we are laughing.

Our soup arrives and the waiter asks about wine. We both shake our heads; even though this is an imaginary conversation we are both reluctant to cloud our minds.

"The first threat directly impacts the second," I say, lifting the melted cheese to reach the soup. "I know I'm simplifying, but I'm convinced that the threats position us," I add, "in ways that create the possibilities of addressing the interconnections between them."

You nod.

"The first threat to our children is the hostile take over the US *public* education system," I say.

"You wrote about this in *Nineteen Clues*," you say. "I read it on the plane."

I say, "'The campaign to destroy those parts of the education system that enrich the lives of students,' Noam Chomsky calls it, 'that interfere with indoctrination, with control, with imposing passivity and obedience.'"[34]

"United Opt Out,[35] Badass Teachers,[36] and Save Our Schools,"[37] you say. "Your explanation of 'BadAss' in *Clues*, it wasn't necessary."

"Across America parents and teachers are organizing," I respond. "Regrettably I left out the websites and blogs of Leonie Haimson[38] and Susan Ohanian.[39] Both have received awards for their activism. Haimson, the John Dewey Award from the United Federation of Teachers, and Ohanian, the George Orwell Award for Distinguished contribution to Honesty and Clarity in Public Language. Fearless. Tireless. Women. If our children are to have a future it will take many more women like them,"

"A few men too," you say. Then in a quiet voice you add. "You know the odds are against all of us."

"But only because men of power lack the will to act," I say. "It's the truth. I'm an old woman and after a lifetime of observation, I'm not impressed by them. Remember I'm also a mother and a grandmother."

"I am too," you say. "And as a mother as well as a scientist it's very clear to me that the world is already experiencing a combination of social and physical catastrophes that could become cataclysmic if we don't act soon."

"I don't have to tell you the second threat to our children is the great acceleration in the changes taking place to the planet," I say. "It's the primary focus of *Nineteen Clues*."

"Humanity is standing at a moment in history when a Great Transformation is needed to respond to the immense threat to the Earth," you respond quoting the Nobel Laureates who wrote in the *Potsdam Memorandum*.[40]

"Society is taking substantial risks by delaying urgent and large-scale action," I respond quoting *The State of the Planet Declaration*, which was the consensus of more than 3,000 scientists at the 2012 *Planet Under Pressure*[41] Conference in London.

"We must show leadership at all levels," you complete the quote, sadly, knowing that the world's leaders have reneged on their responsibilities.

"We must all play our parts," I finish the quote. "We urge the world to grasp this moment and make history."

"Yes, yes, we can recite it every day but it won't make it happen," you say.

You suddenly look jet lagged, but it is only momentary fatigue, because unnoticed by us James Paul Gee has been having lunch with friends in Café Griensteidl, and comes over to say hello as he is leaving the restaurant.

As he approaches I quickly whisper. "Jim's a linguist, known for his approach to discourse analysis, also for his playing and analysis of video games, but not in ways that kids can get tagged." Quickly I whisper, "Jim's a curmudgeon. In his last book *The Anti-Education Era*,[42] he wrote that humans are either marvelously intelligent or amazingly stupid."

"Stupid about climate change," he says, overhearing. He says he's late, but just wants to say hello. "'Climate change is now at a dire point'," he says, "'and we have not yet begun to see the worst of it. It will progressively be a major topic of national discussion at the very least in terms of big storms and the cost of them."[43]

"'The U.S cannot face the future, given climate change and environmental degradation without a changed social structure'," Gee says, looking over to where Murdoch, Klein, and Barber are sitting, "'one that stresses greater equality, more participation, collective intelligence, and indexes of the quality of life beyond economic growth'."

"The issue is on the cusp," he turns and shouts on his way out, "and we need to keep pressing it!"

"Why did you call him a curmudgeon?" you ask, energized by Jim's quick visit.

"He tells it the way he sees it," I say. "It's a complement, of sorts. I appreciate his honesty. In one of his latest books he writes about how smart people – like him and you and me –can be so stupid. It's also one of the questions I'm addressing in the book you are now in, although I would probably rephrase it, and ask – How come people are so smart and power brokers so stupid?"

"You're a curmudgeon too!" you say. "So Gates?"

"Richest man in the world," I say. "Consummate oligarch. A global catastrophe for people and the planet."

"Unsupported opinion, not allowed," you say. "Conditions. Strategies. Planning. Execution."

"He's a double whammy," I say. "His impact on public education in the US is already catastrophic and the cascading effects are cataclysmic for people and the planet."

"Conditions?" you say. "I'm going to be your doctoral examiner!"

"Right!" I say laughing. "At my doctoral defense in 1980 the first question I was asked was 'what is the difference between function and form?' It fits."

"Conditions!"

"I've been documenting the political and ideological conditions since the late 1970's," I respond. "The first account is in *Beginning to Read and the Spin Doctors of Science*[44] in which I debunked the underlying science – known as the Houston Reading Studies that were the basis of the *Reading Excellence Act* in 1998[45] and the *No Child Left Behind Act* in 2001.[46] The political and ideological conditions for what's happening today are based on the fundamental flaws in the original science."

"Fraudulent findings?" you ask. "More than bad science?"

"I would say so," I respond, nodding my head. "There's no other plausible explanation."

"Rationale?"

"Corporate greed," I say, smiling.

"No clichés," you say. "We know it all comes down to money, who has it, who doesn't, who's buying, who's selling."

"The conditions that are rarely mentioned are how we, as a society, use what we know about language and thinking. George Laker calls it framing. An example would be Gee's framing human behavior as either smart or stupid. The idea originates with Charles Frake. I studied his research at Columbia, when I was working on my doctorate."

"How we frame what we know?" you say, one eyebrow raised. "I think the idea was around long before Frake."

"Of course," I respond, feeling foolish. "It's an idea that goes way back."

"A few thousand years," you say, laughing. "But it's more than that isn't it?"

"It's how what we know *frames us*," I say, nodding. "These days what we know is framed by PR firms who use big data. But strip all that away and the underlying assumptions of the reforms that are taking place are fundamentally flawed."

"We're getting somewhere," you say. "Go on.

"This is the research that excites me," I say. "I spend most of my days using language analysis to uncover the relationships between knowledge and experience."

You wave your hand in a small circular gesture to encourage me to continue.

"The condition of learning," I rattle on. "There's an Australian scholar called Brian Cambourne who's spent his life studying children in elementary school classrooms, working with teachers to develop the conditions of learning that support of children's emotional, social, psychological well-being."[47] [48] [49]

"You've been engaged in that work too, haven't you?" you say, "Isn't that the part of the research you've done in schools and in families and communities."

I nod. "Our research is complementary, certainly."

"Including working with children whose language, literacy and learning are impacted by adverse childhood experiences," you say.

I nod, and again you make a circular motion with your hand.

"But it's all gone," I say. "The last hundred years of research across disciplines and professions on how children learn language, learn about language, learn through language, how they actively engage in problem solving, use their imagination, develop their capacity for creative thought, everything we know about human development, it's all gone."

"A bit of an exaggeration don't you think?"

"Yes and no," I say. "The big data guys are totally ignorant of it. They've discarded everything except their own egos."

"I agree with you that it's a problem," you respond. "I read an article in the *Financial Times* on the plane from Stockholm on big data called "Big Mistake", and the multiple comparisons problem."[50]

"I read it too," I say. "There are many problems, not the least the difficulties that arise when the analysis of big data is based on false assumptions about both physical and social phenomena. Nevertheless corporations are jumping on the band wagon, using big data in totally inappropriate and intrusive ways."

You look amused.

"Corporate greed," you say, "is more than a worn out cliché."

"Power, privilege, and profit!"

Now we are both laughing.

"No, but seriously, big data isn't good or bad," you say. "Scientists are also using big data in very powerful and beneficial ways."

"But within the scientific community there are conversations taking place about societal benefits and potential risks," I say, "*and* about standards of conduct. In the US, political and corporate power brokers are not interested in such conversations."

"This is true. Parliamentarians and heads of industry are no different in Europe," you say. "But scientists are interrogating their own practices. We have to. Earth scientists know that if humanity is to survive, if the planet is to remain habitable, it will largely depend on what we do."

Sometimes when you talk I cannot speak. The situation is so dire and the task you have undertaken so formidable.

"Our integrity is critical because our research is so critical to the future of Earth," you say. "There is so little time left, which –" your eyes seem darker, more penetrating, "which, forgive me, makes your concerns about Gates seems to be like a side show."

"Not if it takes center stage," I say. "They've taken over public education in the US. Miseducating children. Indoctrinating them. Kids are becoming passive data processors who won't stand a chance if the predictions for future Earth are correct."

"Is it really that bad?" you ask. "In Denmark there is such an emphasis on child development, on creating supportive learning environments for children, and on the high status of teachers. That is not the case in the US?"

"Gates gave a speech at a National Conference of State Legislatures in July 2009," I say, "in which he lays out his plans for a national curriculum –"

"The Common Core," you say, nodding. "I've read about it." You smile, "*The New York Times* is sold on it."

"Sold out, more like it," I say. "I've stopped reading it."

"After writing *Nineteen Clues*?"

I nod and continue, "At the Conference of State Legislatures Gates rants about the problems with US public schools, and there are many, but Gates' solution is to marketize them. He extols the powerful effects of aligning tests, common standards, and curriculum, that will 'unleash powerful market forces in the service of better teaching.'"[51]

"What I said," Gates says, appearing like the waiter beside our table, "is that 'For the first time, there will be a large uniform base of customers looking at using products that can help every kid learn and every teacher get better. Imagine having the people who create great online video games applying their intelligence to online tools that pull kids in and make algebra and other subjects fun.'"[52] Gates pauses. "The baby artichokes and button mushrooms are on the way," then shakes his head, "you should have had the Griensteidl burger, you could have had one with Gruyere or Roquefort."

"You should have invited him to sit down," you say, after he left.

"I don't eat with aberrant apparitions," I say, shaking my head as Klein moves to the chair besides Barber at table 9, and Gates slides along the bench next to Murdoch where Klein had been sitting.

"He's the reason for all the security," you say, your eyes moving around the restaurant and your head giving an imperceptible nod at the men in suits, one at table 1 near the entrance, another at table 6 near the door to the kitchen. Both men are drinking seltzer.

A waiter who looks familiar arrives with the frites and the rest of the food.

"There is only power," he says, politely, "and those too weak to seek it."[53] [54] Then, bending over us, he says, "Come, the niceties will be observed."[55] [56]

"This is getting too weird," you say. "What's with the quotes?"

"Voldemort," I say. "The whole situation is weird. We're only reflecting it."

You roll your hands again.

"I watched a video yesterday on the official US Department of Education Datapalooza 2012 website.[57] In the video Jose Ferreira of Knewton[58] calls a student a 'schmuck' –"

"A schmuck?" you interject, "Does it mean the same in the US as it does in Europe?"

"I expect so," I say with a shrug, "but it's also used as a pejorative to call someone stupid or foolish, maybe obnoxious, or contemptible. An analysis of Ferreira's talk, and of the presentations of other big data men at the conference makes it clear that they have created their own discourse – they've learned how to move to Center Stage, and Arne Duncan, the US Secretary of Education has given them top billing."

"What Ferreira does is connect the dots. Millions of them," I say, "but they're the wrong dots. He actually has no idea what to do with big data. He trivializes it."

"Knewton," you ask, "what is it exactly?"

"He's selling it," I say. "It's nothing more than an elaborate paint-by-numbers system. Stay within the lines, use the right colors and you get an A."

"Go on."

"If you give this woman here the final right now she'll get an A," Ferreira says, arriving at table 35 and showing us the graphics on his laptop computer. "It's only 14 days into the course. I promise you she'll get an A. You can keep her in that seat if you want, and that's what we've always done now we don't have to"

"Ferreira also says the students in his graphics look like fleas," I say.

"Sub-humans," you say, with a shiver, remembering.

"So let's show you this," Ferreira says. "This is 150 students in one class, and they kind of all look like fleas, but they're all on an individual learning path. Notice that some of them are going really fast, some of them are going really slow, and then they'll all kind of speed up when the test comes. It's kind of like organic and so those different color coded things are like concept clusters. Like some test obviously just happened, that's why they all started working."

You make the time-out sign with your right hand flat on the tips of the fingers on your left hand. "You're inserting transcripts into our imaginary conversation! First Gates and now Ferreira!"

"Is that okay?"

"Highly unusual!"

"Does it work?"

"I think it does?"

"Shall we go on?"

You nod.

"Writing *Keys to the Future* made me reconsider the idea of 'virtual'," I say, considering it necessary to provide an explanation. "That's how this imaginary conversation came about."

You roll your hands again.

"How the word 'virtual' has been coopted to signify events taking place in a digital space," I say. "How the concept has lost its signification for the imaginative world of the mind devoid of technology. "*The Life of the Mind*," Hannah Arendt calls it."

"I get it," you say. "It doesn't matter if you read what you've written in a book or on a tablet, the thoughts that are expressed, the metaphors that are used, and the transcripts which are real, all make up an imaginary conversation that cannot be represented in big data men's virtual world."

"That's it," I say, as Ferreira sits down at the table to make his point.

"And you can look at some of the students and think that poor schmuck is really in a lot of trouble," he says, pointing at another graphic on his computer.

"So where we think we're going with this obviously it's in market right now," Ferreira tells us. "We're going to be in K-12 starting next year and it's an open platform anyone can plug it in and use it by APIs. And where we think we're going with the data side of it, which is the really fun stuff for today, is we think within a few years we'll be able to start predicting great performance."

"So teachers grade persistently year in and year out," Ferreira says, "if that teacher grades consistently, we can match up the student profiles down to the autonomic concept levels versus great performance. We can tell you you're on track to get a B- in this course right now. Either that or if your teacher gets totally inconstant we can't tell you that, but that's another problem."

"If your teacher grades consistently," Ferreira says, shutting his laptop computer, "we can tell you what your grade's going to be based on what you know and how fast you're learning it. But if you do another 30 minutes a day for three days a week you can get it up to an A-."

"We can tell you things like that," he says, as he fades.

You bury your head in your hands

"Overly complicated," I say. "A totally simplistic imposition of a big data model that has no scientific validity or legitimacy that – "

You look as if you might expire.

" – can be undone by one question asked by Noam Chomsky."

You look up, instantly resuscitated.

"Come on!" you say. "What's the question?"

"How can a mosquito fly in the rain?"[59]

"An Earth system science question!" you say. "Let's have some chocolate cake!"

"That's a hard question when you stop to think about it," Chomsky says, as he joins us at table 35 in Café Griensteidl for dessert.

"If something hit a human being with the force of a raindrop hitting a mosquito it would absolutely flatten them immediately," Chomsky tells us. "So how come the mosquito isn't crushed instantly? And how can the mosquito keep flying?"

"If you pursue that question," Chomsky says, "and it is a pretty hard question," he digs his fork into the chocolate cake, "you get into questions of mathematics, physics, and biology, questions that are challenging enough that you want to find an answer."

"Questions about the interrelationships between dynamic complex systems," you say, nodding. "These are the questions that are at the center of Earth system science. How one system influences another, the cascading effects."

"That's what education should be like at every level," Chomsky says, "all the way down to kindergarten, literally. There are kindergarten programs in which, say, each child is given a collection of little items: pebbles, shells, seeds, and thinks like that. Then the class is given the task of finding out which ones are the seeds."

His fork hovers above the chocolate cake.

"It begins with what they call a 'scientific conference'," he says, "the kids talk to each other and they try to figure out which ones are seeds. And of course there is teacher guidance, but the idea is to have the children think it through."

"After a while, they try various experiments and they figure out which ones are the seed," Chomsky continues, as he forks more cake. "At that point, each child is given a magnifying glass and, with the teacher's help, cracks a seed and looks inside and finds the embryo that makes the seed grow. These children learn something-really, not only something about seeds and what makes things grow, but also about how to discover."

"That's what real education is at every level, and that's what ought to be encouraged. That ought to be the purpose of education. It's not to pour information into somebody's head which will then leak out but to be able them to become creative, independent people who can find excitement in discovery and creation and creativity at whatever level or in whatever domain their interests carry them."

Chomsky is no longer at the table and the chocolate cake is also gone, but given that Café Griensteidl is familiar with the theatrical, the waiter brings another piece of cake, with vanilla ice-cream on top.

"When I was little girl my classroom was like the one that Chomsky described," you say. "From the very beginning it was just like that, until I went to university. Learning in that way is how I became a physicist. "

"The possibilities of big data bring benefits as well as risks," I say. "Our ability to organize, visualize, and analyze has taken a quantum leap, if you'll forgive me for the way I'm using the word."

"Appropriately, I think," you say, smiling sadly. "But the potential for great harm to be done to human societies has also taken a quantum leap."

"It's not a sideshow?"

"No," you say. "It's not a sideshow. If the education of our children follows the big data path that Ferreira is on, then the future of humanity is in jeopardy, and the question becomes to which of the great threats to our survival will we first succumb?"

"We both know it won't be one or the other," I say. "Our social and physical worlds are dynamic and inseparable. What happens to the one impacts what happens to the other.

"The cascading effects create tipping points that are both social and physical," you say.

"That's why it's so dangerous when the richest man in the world starts tinkering with both the social and physical systems on which our lives rely, which is what's happening right now."

"Ahh, we're back to Bill Gates, just in time for coffee," you say. "I'm going to have a cappuccino with a triple shot of espresso."

"I'll have one too."

"Coup d'état," you say. "To depose the established government and replace it with a new ruling body, civil or military?"

"I do not use the term lightly," I say, "but based on the analysis of thirty years of data in the Princeton study,[60] the take-away is that the US is now an oligarchy."[61] [62]

"Inferred but not stated," you say. "Multivariate analysis indicates that economic elites and organised groups representing business interests have substantial independent impacts on US government policy," you continue, quoting from the Princeton research report, "while average citizens and mass-based interest groups have little or no independent influence."

"We don't count," I say. "Democracy is an illusion, and imaginary conversation in which the entire nation participates."

"We've talked about the conditions," you say, looking around as if we are in Vienna and it is the 1930's, "as described in your previous research. You can document them historically?"

"In *Keys to the Future* I've analyzed the circumstances in which the coup d'état has taken place," I say. "It's an account of political and economic circumstances that have allowed men like Gates, Murdoch, Coleman, even Ferreira to step into the breach."

"And our imaginary conversation?"

"As I said, it was a new introduction to *Keys to the Future* that took on a life of its own."

"That's happened to me," you say. "In one instance it led to a new discovery."

"What's deeply troublesome," I say, "is that policy makers, who should be making sure the education system is democratic and free of oligarchs and corporate money makers, have opened the doors to K-12 public schools and let them walk right in."

"Strong words!"

"Desperate times!"

"Okay," you say. "We can describe them socially, politically, and ideologically."

"We?"

"Scientists," you say. "All scientific understanding begins with close observation and detailed systematic documentation. Even big data sets start that way."

You raise an eyebrow, and I now know this facial gesture signals some ironic or quirky thought, and you say, "And we know that what is happening is covered by the old cliché of power, privilege, and profit!"

I smile, look up at the ceiling, and then pick up my coffee and take a sip.

"So tell me," you say, "if you write up these descriptions, these narrative accounts, based on your ethnographic research, and couple them with a concomitant discourse and document analysis, can you support your thesis that powerful men like Gates have orchestrated a coup d'état?"

"Strategies, planning, and execution," I say with a smile. "Findings and implications presented here in this imaginary conversation and backed up by the data and analysis presented in *Keys to the Future*."

You clasp your hands and smile.

"Is *Keys to the Future* as iconoclastic as the imaginary conversation?" you ask.

"'fraid so," I say, smiling. "But it's different than this."

You nod.

"I'm interested in linguistic aggression," I say. "The research I find the most compelling is of catastrophic events that take place through the conscious aggressive manipulation of language and thought."

"On the plane I was reading a review by Costica Bradatan[63] of Herta Muller's *Cristina and Her Double*,"[64] you say.

"I've read it too!"

"'Language is like air,'" you say, as if reading the first paragraph of the review. "'You realize how important it is only when it is messed up. Then it can kill you. Those working for totalitarian regimes know this better than anyone else: messing with language can be an efficient mans of political control.'"

"And that is exactly what is happening here," I say. "Linguistic aggression and linguistic occupation which includes well orchestrated surveillance and systematic interrogations.'

"'The battlefield here is not your body,'" you say, again quoting Bradatan's review, "'but your mind and the language you speak'–"

"'Against such a regime you defend yourself not in the street, but in your head,'" I say, finishing the quote. "This is what's happening here in the US, *the land of the free*, the people are not free. Teachers are being slandered, and they're being robbed of their identity. The regime has fabricated negative stereotypes of both parents and teachers, and even *The New York Times* is complicit in this linguistic engineering."

"'Any political disruption of the way language is normally used can in the long run cripple you mentally, socially, and existentially,'" you say, again quoting from the review of Herta Muller's book.

"Corrupts our thinking," I say. "Change the way we use language and you change the way we live in the world," I say, "But the world that's being changed is our children's world. Linguistic aggression and linguistic occupation, which includes well-orchestrated surveillance and systematic interrogations, is taking place in US K-12 public schools."

"How do you even begin to gather the evidence to support a statement like that?" you say.

"Systematically," I say. "But for me what *is* important is not only to counter the linguistic aggression that is taking place, but also to counter by my own language use, the way in which language is being used."

"Ahh, this imaginary conversation we are having!" you say. "It's more than a linguistic contrivance, it's the embodiment of a different view of the mind."

I smile.

"How do you measure something like that?"

"Great question," I say, "an unexpected segue to Michael Barber, 'the mad professor', Peter Wilby at the *The Guardian* calls him, and 'the master of the flow chart.'"[65]

"I called him that in 2011," Wilby says, looking tussle haired and slightly disheveled. He sits down where Chomsky had sat. "You realize it might be lunch time for you in New York, but for me it's dinner time in London and I've already done a day's work."

"I think it was the question I asked about measurement," you say.

"Probably," Wilby says, forking up some frites.

"Be careful," I say. "Barber is sitting over there at that table with Murdoch, Klein and Gates."

"Crikey!" Wilby says, actually something much worse.

"In 2011, I wrote that Barber was Tony Blair's 'backroom boy'," Wilby tells us looking down as he speaks. "He was the head of the Prime Minister's Delivery Unit, for top-down targets across the private sector. He moved in 2005 to the world-renowned management consultancy McKinsey, and its official motto could be his own: 'Everything can be measured, and what is measured can be managed.'"

"That must be the reason you appeared," you say. Anything else you can tell us?"

"The columnist Simon Jenkins called him 'a control freak's control freak,'" Wilby says, clearly wanting to go home for supper. "And the *Mail's* Quentin Letts has compared him to the speaking clock."

"Now Barber and his graphics have gone global," Wilby says. "As McKinsey's hubristically titled 'head of global education practice', he's set up a US Education Delivery Unit." Wilby gives a half smile. "He's also the chief education advisor for Pearson." He looks more quizzical than friendly, as he eyes the people sitting at the tables that are near to us. "Better go," he says. "I don't want to get tagged."

You right hand is flat going up and down on the tips of the fingers on your left hand again.

"Are you serious?" I say. "You're a figment of my imagination, and you're giving me another time out?"

"Yes," you whisper, dropping your hands and hitching your chair closer to the table. "Are you sure you're allowed to do this? Can you bring all these people into your imaginary conversation? Don't you have to abide by some guidelines like imaginary APA? What you think?"

"The reader knows it's an imaginary conversation and that I'm bending genres," I say "All the quotes are referenced at the back of the book."

"Okay," you say. "I'm just making sure you don't get into trouble."

"Thanks," I say, looking serious, "but the whole point is that we've got to use every legitimate means at our disposal to participate in the struggle, and one way or another before this is over we'll all be in trouble. All I have to offer are some thoughts and a few words on the page, so I have to make the most of them."

"Was what Gates said a quote?" you ask, still looking a bit worried.

"About the large customer base eager to buy products?" I ask.

You nod.

"Yes. That's the point isn't it," I say. "This is a satire. He didn't actually play the waiter and recommend the Griensteidl burger with Gruyere or Roquefort. Readers will know that. But all the talk about public education is quoted verbatim."

You roll your eyes.

"I wouldn't quote Gates on education without a reference," I say. "Especially when he's sitting over there having lunch with Michael Barber, Joel Klein, and Rupert Murdoch."

Your head is in your hands.

"You can look," I say. "They can't see you. They're not really there and you're imaginary."

"I know!" you say. "But it seems so real!"

Gates is eating a Griensteidl burger, and is concentrating on his food.

A man sits down at table 8 on the bench seat next to Gates. They were together in Davos and security knows him. They exchange greetings, but do not shake hands.

"It's Jeremy Paxman," you say.

"Listen," I say. "In Davos, Paxman said Gates has made money beyond the dreams of avarice. He asked Gates about the gap between rich and poor."[66]

"When you hear that the poorest half of the world's population own about as much as the 85 richest people in the world, including you of course, does that make you feel uncomfortable?"

"What makes me uncomfortable is that children die," Gates says, and he talks about his foundation's work in Africa.

"But you don't deny the gap between rich and poor seems to have got worse?" Paxton asks, bringing Gates back to his original question.

"No," Gates says. "The gap between rich and poor has not gotten worse, thank goodness."

Paxman looks puzzled, but does not contradict Gates, who continues to talk, and Paxman listens with an odd smile on his face, as if he thinks Gates is demented. He asks Gates why people around the world should spend money on people in poorer countries.

"Well you have to decide do the lives of people in Africa have any value or not?" Gates says. "Does that bother us or not?'

"You could completely alter the picture of the world," Paxman says, "if you went for a genuine redistributed mechanism in taxation."

"You mean like North Korea?" Gates interjects.

"No I don't mean like North Korea," Paxman responds, looking genuinely surprised and laughing a little as he says, "I mean by democratic consent."

Gates has not read the French economist Thomas Piketty's *Capital in the Twenty First Century.*[67]

"R minus G in the 21st century equals wealth *in*-equality," diners chant. "The return of a patrimonial wealth-based society."

"It's the worst of all worlds," Piketty says, stopping by on his way to CUNY.[68]

"How do you persuade people," Paxman asks Gates with a nod to Piketty, "that it is their political or moral duty to pay more taxes in order that there can be some sort of redistribution?"

"You make sure they follow the law," Gates says. "If they don't you put them in jail." He smiles. "Seems to work."

In Café Griensteidl Gates gets a thumbs-down from the diners, and some stand and turn their backs. Others continue to chant "R minus G in the 21st century equals wealth inequality," and diners chant. "The return of a patrimonial wealth-based society!"

Paxman gets ready to leave, but stays in dereference to Piketty who he has also interviewed.

"Between 1990 and 2010, the fortune of Bill Gates," Piketty says, sitting casually on the edge of table 34, facing the diners as if talking to his class at the Paris School of Economics, "the founder of Microsoft, the world leader in operating systems, and the very incarnation of entrepreneurial wealth and number one in *Forbes* ranking for more than ten years," he takes a breath, "increased from $4 billion to $50 billion."

"According to Forbes," you whisper, "Gates net worth is now 78 billion![69] By the time this satire is published he'll probably be worth another billion or even more."

"His wealth has incidentally continued to grow just as rapidly since he has stopped working," Piketty says. "An individual with this level of wealth can easily live magnificently on an amount equivalent to only a few tenths of percent of his capital each year, and he can therefore reinvest nearly all of his income."

Again Piketty pauses.

"Every fortune is partially justified yet potentially excessive," he says. "Outright theft is rare, as is absolute merit."

"No doubt the veritable cult of Bill Gates is an outgrowth of the apparently irrepressible need of modern democratic societies to make sense of inequality," he says. "Nevertheless, it seems to me that Bill Gates also profited from a virtual monopoly on operating systems."

"Furthermore, I believe that Gates's contribution depended on the work of thousands of engineers and scientists doing basic research in electronics and computer science, without whom none of his innovations would have been possible."

Paxman nods. Piketty waves. Gone.

"Time out!" no hands, you actually say it.

"Piketty is under attack," you say. "Maybe you should delete this part of the conversation?"

"Delete Piketty? How could you even suggest it?"

"I'm thinking of you!'

"Irrelevant," I say. We both know it's true.

"Piketty just joined an illustrious group," you say. "So many –"

" –climate scientists under attack –"

" –personally as well as professionally," you say, the hurt in your eyes, "friends of mine. It's brutal – "

" –teachers too. Bullied. Denigrated."

"Chris Giles at the *Financial Times*[70] took advantage of the noise in Piketty's data to try and score," you say.

"Spread doubt," I say. "Quell dissent."

"Giles turned some small differences in interpretation into a big story," you say. "The real story is that the protectors of wealth inequality trashed *Capital*."

"The entire book," I say. "And Giles?"

"Cambridge. Economics degree," you say. "He has the credentials. Bit different than climate deniers' scenario."

"Not really. Same group of powerbrokers on the attack," I say. "The only difference is they are attacking an economist, one of their own."

"What's interesting is that the only aspect of Piketty's research Giles attacks – and a two page spread in the *Financial Times* is an attack – is the increases in wealth inequality over the past few decades".

"Not inequality, the huge gap between rich and poor in US and UK society!"[71]

"In the same edition of *F-T* there are women wearing socks that cost three hundred and forty pounds!" you say. "Five hundred and seventy dollars plus change!"

"They're called 'statement socks'," I say. "They cause bank statement shock!"

"You're losing it!" you say, enjoying the moment.

"The weekend magazine is called '*How to Spend It*,'" I say. "Personal luxuries. Living deluxe. Hot properties starting at ten million. Luxury is an *F-T* protected industry."

"Did you know *F-T's* owned by Pearson?" you say. "Children in US public schools are being trained to produce rich people's bling!"

"Who's losing it?"

"The 85 richest people in the world have as much wealth as the 3.5 billion poorest," you say, quoting Laura Shin in *Forbes*.[72]

"Those stats come from the Oxfam report, '*Working for the Few*,'"[73] I say. "Includes a quote from Louis Brandeis, the US Supreme Court Justice, who said, 'We may have democracy, or we may have wealth concentrated in the hands of a few, but we can't have both.'"

"The consequences of inequality are 'the erosion of democratic governance, the pulling apart of social cohesion, and the vanishing of equal opportunities for all,'" you say, quoting the Oxfam report.

"*Vanishing*, that's the word," I say. "One of my doctoral students, Kathy Olmstead just completed a five year ethnographic study of middle class families with young children in kindergarten and first grade.[74] She's conducted a comparative analysis with the study of middle class families I did thirty five years ago."

"Ah, *life experience*, the verification, *or not*, of statistical data," you say. "Does it support Piketty or Giles?"

"Piketty," I say, "but far more devastating."

"How so?"

"Middle class life of the 1970's is vanishing," I say. "More accurately, vanished!"

"Similarities across time?"

"The joys. The worries. There are many similarities with technology folded in."

"Differences?"

"Social and economic stressors have reached a tipping point," I say. "In Kathy's study both parents have to work, sometimes two jobs, *and* much longer hours. They are all college graduates but both mothers and fathers have lost jobs and had difficulty finding work. One father was told if he wants to keep his job he has to work sixty hours. One mother was recently hospitalized for exhaustion and depression."

"Accelerating societal instability, exacerbated by the increase of inequality occurring in real time and negatively impacting family life," you say. "The contrast between the Gates family and these middle classes families could not be more striking."

"Technology is also making a huge difference," I say. "Seems to enhance the good and exaggerate the bad."

"Good and bad might not be the best terms?" you say.

"Seems to be increasing the gap between learning at home and at school," I say. "Many forms of family communication are now are electronic, but the technology seems more situated than it is as school."

"How so?"

"It's a communicative tool at home, much more so than at school, where –" I hesitate searching for an analogy, "it's as if the use of technology is on the spectrum."

"Autistic?"

"Exactly. Highly repetitive. Skill and drill. Pre-test. Test," I say. "Teachers are not allowed to read the tests their students take and they don't get the test results back. Just the scores. Communication is not even a consideration."

"Pearson," you say.

"And Gates!" I say. "A cataclysmic combination!"

Gates, oblivious to the conversation, to the Piketty attacks, to the negative views of his critics, or to his own gaffes, turns and talks to

Murdoch, Klein and Barber at table 9 about US K-12 education. It's a conversation that he had at Harvard in 2013.[75]

We pick it up at the point at which he negates the idea of small changes in the US K-12 education system, and talks about "doing things that are high risk, but at some point might have a big impact".

Gates talks about how he and his wife Melinda reached decisions about the future of K-12 public education in US.

"It's like raising kids," he says. "You talk and talk, there's a quid pro quo, and somehow it all works out."

"It's never been that difficult," he says. "We're on different trips and it's a lot of fun to talk about it."

Thumbs down. Backs turn. Security talks into their lapels. Gates continues talking.

"In education if you are trying to improve the K-12 personnel system," he says, "because it is subject to so many uncertainties including school boards, political processes, union negotiations, and the desire to maintain the status quo –"

" – if you said to me, 'Are we making progress on that one or not?', I could talk for a long time, but I wouldn't be able to give you a number, and so the very risk of it and the complexity of the system change that's necessary makes that tougher to measure."

"I am a total fan of measurement," he says, "where it can be done but the degree that would drive you to low risk things and steer you away from trying to improve K-12 then the fetish towards measurement can be taken too far."

"It would be great if our education stuff works," he says, "but that we won't know for probably a decade."

"'The *very risk* of it'?" you say.

"'It would be great *if* our education stuff works'?" I say.

"'But that we *won't know* for probably a decade'!"

I close my eyes and shake my head.

'He's taking risks with the education of more than 50 million children in US public schools," you whisper.

"He's holding their future, *their lives*, in his hand," I say, "and he's prepared to risk all 50 million of them on what amounts to nothing more than a game of poker."

Two thumbs down. Security is up. A nod from Gates and they are gone.

Klein is leaning back in his chair. He's saying something to Murdoch, who is leaning forward arms on the table, the way he did at the when he gave evidence, in April 25, 2012, at the Levinson Inquiry into the News Corp hacking scandal in which a murdered child's phone was hacked. The Murdoch scandal killed the UK *News of the World* and his planned take-over of the UK BSkyB satellite network. He looks remarkably the same, same bright blue tie that he wore during his testimony at which he was told, "there is a perception that he uses his influence impermissibly".[76]

"'This is the most humble day of my life,' Murdoch said," you say, repeating his words verbatim from the 2011 UK Parliament Committee Hearing.[77] [78]

"I was in London a year later," I say, "at the time of the Levinson Inquiry."

"It was just after the 2012 *Planet Under Pressure*," you say. "I was there too."

"It was compelling," I say. "A precious week in London and I spent it watching Murdoch testify."

"I remember," you say. "A humbling week."

"It might well have been for Murdoch, but that doesn't negate the very serious nature of the charges brought against him, nor does it minimize the charges that should be brought against the public officials in the US, who have placed in his keeping confidential information collected about children in US public schools."

"You'll have to make the connection for me," you say.

"It's the reason they're all at that table," I say. "Gates put up over one hundred million dollars to establish a non-profit that was called inBloom, that would be used to upload and store confidential data on children in US K-12 public schools. The information was going to be stored on a data cloud run by Amazon, wait for it, with an operating system provided by Wireless/Amplify, which is a Murdoch corporation headed up by run by Joel Klein. Without parental consent, very personal information about children and their families was going to be made available to "approved" software companies and other for-profit vendors."[79] [80]

"A corporate feeding frenzy," you say. "And parents protested?"

"Yes, Leonie Haimson led the charge,"[81] [82] I say. "Gates lost. So did Murdoch."

"A parent uprising against the coup d'état," you say. "Establishes precedence!"

"Perhaps leading to a larger rebellion," I say. "There are so many different angles to this, but it's important to note that at the time Murdoch's company Wireless/Amplify was signing the contract to keep the data on US public school children he was being censured in the UK for hacking the phone of a child who was brutally murdered."

"I remember John Whittingdale, one of the MP's in the parliamentary investigation of the British House of Commons," you say, "stating that Murdoch had misled the committee, and that he 'failed to produce documents that would have revealed the truth'. And Tom Watson, another MP, stating that 'in the view of the majority of committee members Rupert Murdoch is not fit to run an international company.'"[83]

"Watson also said," I add, "'Many of the hacking victims have still not been informed about what was done to them and Rupert Murdoch has not said his last apology to the families of murdered children.' Watson said, 'These people corrupted our country they bought shame on our police force and our parliament they lied and cheated blackmailed and bullied and we should all be ashamed when we think how we cowered before them for so long.'"

"What do you take from that?" you ask.

"We'll never know all the ins and outs," I say, "but Murdoch has unprecedented power. There are several reliable sources that quote Murdoch saying, 'When you are the monopoly supplier, you are inclined to dictate',[84] [85] but I have not found a video of his actually speaking the words."

"Control opinion and you control the world?"

"Something like that," I say. "And when media moguls and oligarchs join forces then there is a real danger that what's left of social contracts made in the two decades after the Second World War will be destroyed --"

" – it's already happening."

"And public education, community colleges, state universities are all in jeopardy"

"There are enough open source documents that indicate Gates, Klein, Murdoch and Pearson are all intricately connected, and that there are questions of legality and illegality in some of these connections."

"And Michael Barber?" you ask. "Where is he in all this?"

"There are many different connections. As far as I know, nothing illegal," I say. "Although he just received two hundred and fifty thousand dollars from the Gates Foundation for a report he wrote for the Massachusetts Business Alliance of his vision of "Education in Massachusetts in the Next 20 Years"[86] in which he plagiarized the *Boston Globe*."[87]

"An isolated oversight," Barber says, coming over and sitting at table 35 where Chomsky had sat.

"Everything else has been meticulously done in other parts of the report," he says. He looks from one to the other of us and smiles benignly. "So what are you up to over here?"

"A school assignment actually," I say. "Our task is to have an imaginary conversation about the two threats to our children that impact every aspect of their present and future lives."

"Well, I think I can help you with that," Barber says. "I spoke about this at Nesta in the UK, December, 2012."[88]

"Bring on the Whole System Global Education Revolution!" I say, repeating the title of Barber's talk, "I watched the video. Actually transcribed it and conducted a discourse analysis, and then compared it with other speeches you've given and some of the papers you've written."

"You have been busy!"

"I'm interested in your introduction," I say, "in which you talked about the big picture of your arguments and about 'the state of the world'."

Barber gives a wise man nod.

"You said you were worrying about two things, one being the set of challenges facing humanity—"

"When you start adding up the conflicts," Barber says, interrupting, "and the gaps of wealth and poverty, the environmental challenge, the pace of economic growth and the pressure that puts on the planet, the fact there are going to be nine billion people on the planet by 2050."

His fingers hover over the roasted mushrooms and he pushes one of them aside before picking one up with his thumb and forefinger and placing it in his mouth.

"You put all that together and then you add in nasty dangerous things like conflict, weapons of mass destruction, terrorism," he says. "And we began to think about that, and we remembered a story Isaac Asimov wrote called *Nightfall*."[89]

Barber's hand hovers again over the mushrooms.

"It's about an imaginary planet with twelve suns so it's daylight all the time and every twelve suns and everybody is – and all goes well and then one time there is a perfect eclipse of all twelve suns and nightfall comes and the planet's civilization comes to an end –"

"Can I stop you right there," you say, with the palm of your hand towards Barber. "That's not how I remember the story. All is *not* going well. The story is about the leader of a cult and his followers, there's a newspaperman, and then there's the public."

Barber does not respond.

"Can he hear me?" you ask, irritated that Barber is ignoring you.

I shake my head.

"Poetic license," you say. "I suppose there's no script and you're being careful not to put words in Barber's mouth." Now you're laughing. "Just mushrooms!"

"There are parallels though," I say, responding to your objection to Barber's interpretation of *Nightfall*. "You could argue that Asimov wrote a prophetic story. Pearson has all the characteristics of a cult, News Corp has been officially censured for the manipulation of the media, the people are in 'an ugly humor' with Pearson, and," I say, looking directly at Barber, "as Asimov writes, 'Johnny Public doesn't believe you.'"

Through the window we can see some people gathering in the sunshine. They are standing, as if waiting for a bus, but some of them have big placards that they are writing on.

"When you give this speech again, you might refer to Italo Calvino's *Daughters of the Moon*,[90] which would work much better and is also a marvelous story," you say.

"Then we were thinking," Barber continues his *Oceans* talk at Nesta, "where is the leadership around the world to solve all these problems and we started running around the world looking for bold. Imaginative, strategic leadership and we struggled. We ran around the world –" and he refers to Ian Bremmer's work and the idea of a G-Zero."[91]

"And so the beginning of our argument," Barber quickly goes on, "is that unless we get something changed in the next 50 years we face this rather frightening constellation of *Nightfall* with G-Zero."

He gestures towards the window. "Something's happening out there."

"And then you think," Barber says, back to his topic, "well we are supposed to be writing about education here but we've got a bit carried away. This is important stuff but then you ask where global leadership comes from?"

He gives a history lesson on Britain's leadership position, in trade and economic growth, and then focuses on the beginning of the 21st century and how the neo-cons in the US missed the big story and got it wrong. He asks how societies would need to change to generate the global leadership.

"Are you saying that Pearson is going to decide how societies need to change?" I ask. Isn't that a decision for the people in whatever society you are talking about to decide?" Or is it now the Pearson Empire rather than the British Empire? Colonial rule? Is Pearson picking up where Queen Victoria left off?"

"What would they need to do with their economies?" he asks, not hearing me.

You glance over at the windows. The people have become a huge throng, shadowy figures holding up signs and placards are blocking out the sun.

"What would they have to do with their education system?" Barber continues. "Would they need a more innovative society? Well, probably they would." He talks of "the need in global leadership for people who are well-educated, competent, driven imaginative, you need people who are inquisitive and so on and we looked at it at the level of the team."

"On the team we thought about it a lot because on our own team at Pearson we have tried to construct this. We've used the research to construct the team." Barber has practiced his speech and has clearly given it many times before. "And at the end of having put all this together we were thinking, actually, although the economic miracle of the Pacific Asian Societies over the past fifty years is pretty remarkable, in some ways unprecedented in human history, what they have got to do in the next fifty years isn't the same, they can't do more of the same, because it won't work, so then you say what do they need to do to their education systems to change them to make them more effective."

"This is your imaginary conversation!" you whisper to me, "interrupt him!"

"I can't!" I say. "It's important that we get it. Pearson is British to the core. You've gotta read the *Oceans of Innovation* report.[92] The devil is in the details. On the face of it the report was written for the UK "Institute for Public Policy Research", but all three authors were working for Pearson at the time the report was prepared. It's important that we get it. Prior to signing on with Pearson, Barber was head of McKinsey's Global Education Practice, and his two co-authors were both "consultants" at McKinsey.

"McKinsey not only consults for Pearson but also the *Financial Times*," you say. "Statement socks!"

"Spread doubt."

"Quell dissent!"

"Barber's interpretation of PISA is clouded by class and has been totally undermined by people like David Berliner." I smile, knowing I am being insufferable, and say, "and also by me." Then more seriously, "Just look at the map in the *Oceans* report that Barber pulled from *Urban World: Cities and the Rise of the Consuming Class –*"[93]

" – that report is published by McKinsey."

"Barber is an upper class Brit and a history teacher to boot – that's *British* history. He is steeped in a history of colonial rule and he doesn't even know it. In *Oceans* he writes of the "shift in the world's economic centre of gravity –"

"A sobering way to look at this transformation," Barber says, unaware of the criticism that is being made of the national ethos of English upper class exceptionalism, "especially for any Westerner at risk of suffering hubris, is to see it in the context of very long historical trends. Either way, the rise of China and Pacific Asia, and the implications this has for global leadership, is a major transformation of global leadership that cannot be ignored."

"Very clever," you say. "Capitalize on the myth of the superiority of the Brit ruling classes. Play on the fears of Superpowers that were once British colonies because deep down they are still just that, colonial in their thinking."

"It's mad," I say. "It's bad. And, it's brilliant."[94] [95]

"Pearson is building an Empire," you say. "According to Barber there are no leaders in the world and so Pearson is going to fill that leadership role with dominions, *colonies*, dependencies, trusts, territories, and protectorates. Pearson is going to rule the world and save the planet!"

"Have you looked outside?" you ask. "I'm just trying to tell you that the public is in an ugly humor," you whisper, glancing at the window and quoting Asimov in *Nightfall*. "That anger might take shape into something serious!"

Barber continues talking. He doesn't notice it is getting darker and he does not hear us. He has reached the part in his speech where he talks about the global student rankings of TIMSS and PISA.

"What we've done is gather all the different rankings in one data base and all the info measures we could get globally so we put these big data sets together," Barber says. "And you can play about in the big data."

He talks about Singapore and Hong Kong and "systems that succeed".

"And then you say," Barber continues, "well maybe that's enough and it has worked really remarkably well in the last fifty years but what would they need to do differently in the next fifty years?"

"And I was saying," Barber goes on, "Well those international comparisons are good and they measure knowledge and application of skills but do they measure all the things you want to generate the kind of society that is going to solve all the problems I was talking about at the beginning?"

"And when I talk about innovation," Barber continues, "I don't just mean gadgets and technology, I mean changing the way our society works, so what kind of students and what set of standards should we expect?"

"Stop him!"

"Not yet!" I whisper. "Barber talking is Pearson thinking out loud. He is laying out the company's vision for Pearson to usurp governments."

"K stands for knowledge, T stands for think, and L for learning," Barber says. He talks of making explicit the ways of thinking so "you are doing it better". He talks about L for leadership.

"And here we mean," Barber says, "not just leading big organizations, although that is important, we mean in your community learning how to persuade people are really important skills."

"How many schools really know which students are getting K, T, and L?" he says, sounding slightly maniacal. "How many times does the head teacher of a school sit with the school roll and the management team and go through every child and say 'Is he getting L?' 'Is she getting L?'"

He stops suddenly and looks over to where Murdoch and Klein were sitting. "They've gone without me," he says, not seeming surprised. He looks out the window.

The placards are so thick there is no light. The shadowy figures are indistinguishable from one another, somehow they have lost their individuality and merged into a continuous shadowy mass.[96] Outside it is dark enough to be night, and there is a murmuring, voices rising and falling, not quite loud enough for the words to be heard.

"We must be going to have a storm," Barber says, "Sounds like thunder rolling across the Hudson River from New Jersey."

Suddenly a woman bursts into the restaurant and slams the door. It has taken her a few minutes to make her way through the crowd, and although she is elegantly dressed she is totally disheveled. She rearranges the strands of hair that have fallen forward covering her face, smoothes her suit jacket, and walks with authority, as if taking command of the situation, as if taking command of the situation.

"Michael," she says, walking over to where we are sitting at table 35, "you could have called the office or sent a text."

Barber stands and she gestures for him to join her at table 34.

"Sarah Montague," the woman says, looking at you and then me as she holds out her hand. "BBC. I interviewed Michael for *Hardtalk*.[97] I presume that's why I am here?"

"The video has been removed from the BBC website," I say. "But after a search I found the podcast and transcribed it."

"There is a five minute clip from the interview on Pearson's website," Montague says.

"Very pro Pearson," I say. "I thought we might run through the rest of the interview? Or at least the first part which has been removed from all the sites I checked?"

"Look," Barber says, "I really have to go. I don't like the look of that crowd. It's growing into an angry mob."

"I wouldn't go out there," Montague says. "I'd join in if I was you. Not much else you can do." She looks around and gestures to a waiter. "Americano. Maybe some biscotti?" The waiter hurries off.

Montague gets it. She introduces Barber, who is looking a little flushed, and she says he is now working for the international company Pearson. Some of the people at nearby tables, who are used to theatrical performances and are worried about going outside, decide to stay and turn their chairs to listen to the interview.

"Pearson has announced it will invest millions in private schools for the world's poorest families," Montague says, takes a sip of her Americano, quite relaxed and comfortable with her impromptu audience.

"Is that the right way to tackle the problem?" she asks. "Or could it undermine what governments are trying to do? Pearson has called this the Affordable Learning Fund?"

"Tell us how it is going to work," Montague instructs Barber.

"The idea is to invest 15 million dollars over the next few years in chains of low cost private schools in the developing world," Barber says, sounding much more humble than he did when he was expounding on Pearson saving the world, "chains that are aimed at the poorest families in the developing world to provide education for their children."

"If governments are going to solve the problem of education for families in the developing world," he says, back on familiar ground, "we have to have the government systems improving and we have to invest in low cost private schools."

"First of all 15 million dollars is not very much money," Montague says.

"Right," Barber responds sounding eager to agree. "But it will go a long way to get started and this is a very, to use the economic jargon, this is an immature market and we think taken to scale we can get large chains of school that are consistent and higher quality."

"And that are run by Pearson?" Montague follows up, just as the lights are turned up.

"No, no, no," Barber says, reassuringly. "We'll be minority investors in this so we are going to back entrepreneurs out there in India Pakistan or Africa."

"You talk about a private school in places like Africa," Montague states, "and one presumes this is going to be for the middle classes. This can't really be for the millions of children who are struggling to get an education, who are those whose families are perhaps living on less than a dollar a day?"

"On the contrary," Barber again reassures her. "These are schools for very poor people at the lowest level three or four dollars a month at the higher level eight, nine, ten dollars a month."

"And you are saying to go to it a family would pay three dollars a month?"

"That's the low, very lowest level end of the spectrum, yes," Barber says, sounding less convincing. "And if you think about it as a day's wages for a laborer for a month's schooling, this is really low cost education."

"It's still a lot though isn't it," Montague quickly comes back, "that question of when you are earning a dollar a day?"

Chairs scrape as the people having lunch move closer to table 34. Some of the restaurant staff come over. Someone whispers, "It's like a total eclipse of the sun." For a time the murmuring of the protesters outside on 72th Street had got much louder, but now it is less than a hum.

"Are there hidden costs in which you are investing?" Montague asks.

"Well," Barber says, "in the first investment we have made, which is in Ghana, there are no hidden costs. The children pay daily. They walk into the school daily. They have a wristband that clicks their attendance."

"Tagged," you whisper.

"They pay literally daily," Barber says, "that's in consultation with the parents in the area. Rather than pay a lump sum, they would rather pay a small amount daily, and the daily fee includes a daily meal, the uniform, the book, everything and they pay for about two hundred days a year and they get ten free days a year."

It seems lighter. The people outside the restaurant are putting their signs and placards on the ground, their heads are bent forward as if they are praying, and audible inside the restaurant are the words "the book", but not just "the book" but "*the* book" with the emphasis on the singular definite article, and "the *book*?" with the emphasis on the singularity of the noun as the word becomes a question, "*one* book?"

"For Pearson this is about making money isn't it," Montague says, so totally absorbed by her interview of Barber that she could be in a BBC studio in London and not Café Griensteidl in New York.

"For Pearson," Barber says, speaking slowly and deliberately, "it is about demonstrating that for profit education can provide high quality at low cost for poor people across the developing world."

"For profit," Montague says. "It's about –"

"It's absolutely about profit," Barber says, and the murmur outside is clearly audible, but he doesn't hear it. "But get this right. It's important to demonstrate profit because we want other investors to come in. It's not a huge part, as you yourself mentioned. It is a relatively small amount of money, but we want to demonstrate for-profit education can work in the developing world. We see a huge need."

"And so you need to show," Montague says, pronouncing each word with perfect upper class diction, "that for profit works, and for Pearson that profit will go back to Pearson's shareholders."

"Well the profit would be made by the schools," Barber says, his diction less declarative, "and Pearson would gain, if at some point we sold our stake back to the school –"

Barber keeps talking and Montague interrupts.

"It's really important," she says. "Sorry. Forgive me. I just want to nail down how this works so people can understand. You put this money in expecting that at some point in the future you'll get a capital gain from it over the years because you will sell it on to another investor?"

"Maybe, ten years down the road," Barber says. "Maybe back to the people, the owners of the school, maybe another investor who knows."

"But you are not expecting a dividend?"

"We are not trying to get a monthly return or an annual return –"

"And is part of the deal that they should buy Pearson, material, text books, training, exam systems?" Montague asks.

"No," Barber says.

"Because Pearson is a vast global enterprise," Montague says, and what could be a question, sounds more like a declarative sentence.

"It's a big FTSE 100 company absolutely," Barber responds, the pride clearly audible.

"And there is no quid pro quo that we will put this money in but we expect this in return?" Montague asks.

"No," Barber is decisive, and then equivocates. "I mean if that is what the school wanted to do they could do that but we are not making it a quid pro quo, no."

"You make the point that it is patronizing to suggest that the poorest in the world shouldn't have a choice," Montague says. "Trouble is there is an argument that what you are doing is undermining the government system. Joseph O'Reilly, who is head of education at *Save the Children*, has stated that it diverts attention away from the problem, that even if you have this sector at a relatively low cost, it is not doing anything to address the more fundamental problem –"

Barber rationalizes private schools, but stresses that he has worked for government. "I love government, government is important, it is a big part of the solution" he says. He continues, then falls back on a statement he made at Nesta.

"It's really easy in the education debate to fall into false dichotomies," Barber says. It's an argument breaker that has worked in other contexts but not with Montague. "The road to hell is paved with false dichotomies in education. We have to improve government systems Pearson will work with governments to do that."

Barber gives every indication he thinks he is on solid ground.

"But ideally would the state be providing education and would they be providing it for free?" Montague asks, shaking his argument. "Is that the ideal world?

"I would love in an ideal world that government provided a good quality education that everybody could go to if they wanted," Barber says. "But I would also like, in an ideal world, a person who wanted to choose another school if they wanted. I am in favor of choice –"

"It's just strange," Montague picking up on the road to hell, "I know you don't like what you call false dichotomies and I am trying to see how it is false, when what you are actually doing is to – is to expand a market in for-profit education."

"And there will be some," Montague continue, "I mean, there are people who actually say, what are you trying to do here," for the first time she searches for the right way to say what she wants to say, "you are getting to the point, when you are effectively going to control education, and get to a point when a government will say, 'Let's contract it out to Pearson."

"Well governments may well get to contracting out education to for-profit companies at some point," Barber says, seemingly oblivious to why that is a problem, "and some governments already do that. But the most important thing is instead of thinking, 'all we've got to do is fix the government sector', they should ask the question, 'how should we get all the children in our country or our province a good education?' It really is urgent –"

Montague interrupts as Barber repeats several times that there are going to be nine billion on the planet by the middle of the 21st century.

"Okay," Montague says, "but if you are to win the argument people need to know what the intention, what Pearson's goals are. Diane Ravitch –"[98]

There are cheers outside; people are shouting, and clapping.

"Diane! Diane!" the people shout.

"What's happening?" you whisper. You follow my eyes as they move from one diner to another sitting on chairs crammed together. Sound turned off, they are discretely, unobtrusively, holding their phones in their laps, and they are making videos of Montague's *Hardtalk* interview of Barber. Other diners are standing behind those who are seated holding up their phones with no worries of discretion getting videos from every side full frontal of Montague, full frontal of Barber, while others are taking photographs from every angle.

"Diane Ravitch," Montague says, "who is an influential American historian and commentator –"

"Diane!" the crowd shouts. The diners in Griensteidl are smiling, sending Tweets. Their videos are being live streamed, not only to the crowd outside, but to parents and teachers across the US.

Montague turns and looks out the window. A woman who has pulled her chair up close to Montague shows her a photo sent to her by a friend outside of the people gathered there holding up a hastily written sign "Pearson never consulted us!"

"Save our children" the crowd chants, "Opt out! Save our school! Pearson broke the golden rule!"

"They are parents and teachers," the woman whispers to Montague.

Montague nods and continues without missing a beat.

"I suppose the goal is to get the business up and running," she says, "then get government to foot the bill as it outsources education to Pearson?"

Barber stammers as he did in the studio in London when Montague originally asked the same question, but now in New York the situation is much more complicated and half his mind is on his escape.

"You are perfectly safe," I whisper to him. "This is imaginary."

"Well," Barber says looking a little flushed, "this implies there is some sort of global domination by Pearson this is completely misunderstanding this is, this is, err, --"

"The masters of mankind are multinational corporations and financial institutions," Chomsky says, reappearing and looking at Barber from the lectern at which Chomsky was standing in the video that suddenly came to mind.[99] [100] "It helps explain why the State-Corporate complex is indeed a threat to freedom and in fact even to survival," he says, before fading with a gentle nod to the diners in Café Griensteidl.

"Education around the world is a vast, err, enterprise with more and more money going in, Barber says, back on message, unaware that Chomsky has just outed him. "Governments, I think for the foreseeable future, will be, and should be the major provider of education, that's as it should be."

"And so who are you selling on to in seven years?"

"I work with governments all the time," Barber says, "to help them I improve their education systems."

"Diane Ravitch –"

Again the cheers, the crowd is getting louder, murmurs have become audible, a steady hum, with occasional shouts of "No more Pearson in our school, Pearson broke the golden rule" and "No more, Common Core!"

"Diane Ravitch again questions this," Montague says again, determined to finish the interview, "she writes, 'there must certainly be some questions raised about the cultural, political, and ideological content of the education that is provided, what kinds of teachers in the three dollar a month schools.'"

"The teachers will be good young people who turn up and do a good job," Barber responds, seeming to be unaware of the inadequacy of his answer.

"No more Pearson in our school!" the chanting reaches a crescendo.

"Pearson broke the golden rule!"

"Democratize! Don't colonize!"

"My son draws boxes with bars," a mother shouts, "and says schools are prisons!"

"Today was tough," a teacher says, who has come inside. "The test was hard. There was a noticeable change in climate at school. Very high stress. The crisis team seemed everywhere. Such torture for these kids! We had at least three students rip up tests, and one student who wrote obscenities on his answer sheet then ate part of it so he wouldn't get in trouble. Poor kid ate his paper!"

"My kids used to love math," Louis C.K. says, from the table 11 in Griensteidl where he's been watching the scene. "Now it makes them cry. Thanks standardized testing and common core!"[101]

"I trust a teacher over Pearson," he says.

"Thirty three thousand parents agree," a diner shouts, "opted their children out of the misery!"

"No more Pearson in our school!" the chanting reaches a crescendo.

"Pearson broke the golden rule!"

Then silence. The crowd is anticipating Montague's next question.

"What if we don't get it right?" Montague asks, with perfect diction, each word loaded, each sound, each syllable, firing.

"Well if you are an investor sometimes –" Barber says, in colonizer mode, oblivious to the significance of the question.

"I didn't mean from that point of view," Montague says.

Hardtalk is what the show is about – that well-worded moment when the ugly side of "benevolence" appears, when the nefarious practice, the avarice, the greed, is revealed.

In Café Griensteidl the diners send Barber's "investor" comment in multiple Tweets and as well as video clips. Outside the protesters fingers and thumbs are moving furiously in one Tweet after another.

At home resting her injured knee, Ravitch picks up the Tweets and types "Breaking News", and her followers read her blog as far away as Singapore and Hong Kong. Encrypted, the blog is sent on to China where conversations take place. Harsh questions are asked about who is responsible for Pearson's plans to colonize Asia and the Pacific Rim.

In the US, where parents and teachers read Ravitch and other bloggers pick up the feeds, a hundred and fifty education bloggers give their own take on the story. Analysis and commentary by Ohanian, Krashen,[102] Garrison,[103] McDermott,[104] and Cody[105] is quickly uploaded, and their followers watch the videos and read the Tweets. Then, in turn, Ravitch resends their blogs to a million more teachers who quickly re-Tweet.

Meetings are arranged between men in high places to discuss how Barber and Pearson got it so wrong and try to contain the damage of a billion Tweets of "Save our children. Save our school. Pearson broke the golden rule."

"Thank you," I say to Montague.

"My pleasure," she says. "Is Diane Ravitch outside? I think I'll say hello to her."

"Another time," I say. "I think she is busy writing her blog, but I am sure she would agree to be interviewed on *Hardtalk*, if you invite her."

"Good idea," Montague says, "Why not." She holds out her hand as her image fades, and all that is left in her perfect diction are the words, "It's been a pleasure."

"I've got to go too," Barber says. "You did say this is just an imaginary conversation?"

"Yes," I say. "No YouTubes or Tweets." I hold out my hand. "But if you don't mind there is one last question I'd like to ask you."

"Why not," Barber says, with a shrug, but without shaking hands.

"It's about *Nightfall*," I say. "Isaac Asimov's short story. There are only six suns."

"What?" Barber looks confused.

"When you spoke to Nesta you said there are twelve suns."

"Six? Twelve? Does it matter?" Barber asks, looking confused. There is nothing before him except shadows. The very floor beneath his feet lacks substance.

"It matters a lot," I say.

Barber looks confused, as the last thread of sunlight shining through the window thins out and snaps.[106]

There is a strange silence outside.[107] Inside diners continue to video, take photos, fingers are moving rapidly and so are thumbs as multiple Tweets and texts are also sent.

"In *Nightfall*," I say, quoting from the end of Asimov's story, "Thirty thousand mighty suns shone down in a soul-searing splendor that was more frighteningly cold in its awful indifference than the bitter wind that shivered across the cold, horribly bleak world."

Barber staggers, leaving the imaginary conversation, and finds himself in *Nightfall*. "For this is the Dark – the Dark and the Cold and the Doom. The bright walls of the universe are shattering and their awful Black fragments are falling ..."[108]

"Stars – all the Stars –" you quote, "we didn't know at all."

"We didn't know anything," I say, still quoting. "We thought six stars in a universe is something the Stars didn't notice is Darkness forever and ever and ever and the walls are breaking in and we didn't know we couldn't know and anything –"

"What are you saying?" Barber asks. "I don't understand?"

"That's precisely the point," I say. "You got it wrong. You made *Nightfall* a metaphor for what is happening to the planet and you linked it to the leadership- around the world, but if you got *Nightfall* wrong what does that tell us about your understanding of the leadership around the world?"

"It's an important question," you say. "If I was the leader of a country in Asia or the Pacific Rim, or here in the US in a Statehouse, or inside the Beltway in Washington, DC, I would be worried that the great mind of the global company that is planning to educate the world leaders of the 21st century doesn't know what he is talking about."

"It reveals the fallibility of Pearson's thinking," I say, "and the falseness of the foundation on which the rationale for the company's Whole System Global Education Revolution rests."

Around the Earth the videos and Tweets go out.

"Pearson failed the test!"

"Rule Britannia, no longer rules the waves!" the protesters video and Tweet.

"Pearson never, never, ever shall be-e- saved!"[109]

*In which nine white men from Oxford and Harvard align
themselves in such a way that they have the power to
aggressively pursue a Whole System Global Education
Revolution requiring acts of resistance and consciousness
raising, as we confront our acquiescence to their tyranny*

ACT THREE

"I wish I'd been here for all the excitement," you say, returning after your absence in the Second Act. You sit in the seat at table 35 that was occupied a few moments ago by the Danish physicist who has left for the *Future Earth* meeting at the UN.

"Not sure why I had to leave after Act One," you say.

"Makes the writing too complicated," I say, smiling. "Glad you are back."

"Did Barber really say, 'The road to hell is paved with false dichotomies in education'?" You look incredulous. "And, 'We have to improve government systems,' and 'Pearson will work with governments to do that'?"

"He did," I say. "Twice. When he spoke at Nesta and when he was interviewed for *Hardtalk* by Montague."

"And Pearson is going educate the leaders of Asia and the Pacific Rim?" you say, breathlessly recapping the conversation that has taken place, "*and* the future leaders of the U-S-A? *and* the U-K? *and* fix Africa? I'm not sure Africa wants to be fixed by a bunch of Brits! They were the ones who messed it up in the first place!"

"I'm not sure I would put it exactly like that," I say.

"Don't forget I am a figment of your imagination!"

The Pearson plan is to make the Whole System Global Education Revolution irreversible. And it will be as irreversible and catastrophic as climate change.

The diners at the table 24 are talking about the NY Philharmonic and the upcoming plans for the Biennial. A woman with black lined eyes is holding up her iPad so that the rest of the people at her table can see an image of Matthew Muckey playing his trumpet against a backdrop of moonlight on water.

"It's such a joyful image of the world," the woman says.

"It's magnificent," the man sitting next to her says. "Most of all, its playful." The man looks like Dumbledore. He has long grey hair tied back, a long grey beard, and he is looking through a pair of ancient gold-framed spectacles.

"'Ah, music'!" he says, wiping his eyes. "'A magic beyond all we do here!' Sometimes there are no words. Just images and sounds."[110][111]

"Here's the one of Sumire Kudo," the woman says, and she holds out her iPad to the man and he takes it and sits for a long time looking with tears in his eyes at the evocation of Kudo playing her violin in the middle of a woodland scene.

"What's with the Philharmonic?" you whisper.

"The road to heaven," I say, laughing, and then quickly add that I am not serious. "I'm responding to Barber's false dichotomies," I add. "The images are symbolic of the human spirit. They are imagined representations, no more real than this conversation, but they are vitally important, nevertheless."

"I'm waiting for Maya Angelou to appear," you say, looking around

Café Griensteidl as if you really think she might join us.

"Every time you open a book," I say. "All the children's authors who wrote to the President appear, *and* Toni Morrison, and great philosophers too, Hannah Arendt and Maxine Greene."

"Yes!" you say. "All of them, all our imaginary friends in the pages of books, that the drudgery of the Whole System Global Education Revolution is taking away."

"The *Sovereignty of Good*,"[112] I say, thinking of Iris Murdoch, and then Simone Weil and "*Gravity and Grace*."[113]

"The struggle for good against the human capacity for evil," you say. "Barber, Murdoch, Klein, Coleman –",

"– Gates –"

"– and Arne Duncan?" you say. "What about Arne?"

Yes, Duncan. Can't leave him out," I say. Let's finish off Barber first."

"I agree with your friend from Denmark that Barber should change his story from Asimov's *Nightfall* to Calvino's *The Daughters of the Moon*?"

I nod. Smiling. Like me you know the story well.

"'The Moon is old," you say, "'pitted with holes, worn out. Rolling around naked through the skies'–"

"And Calvino describes the Moon and Earth as mirror images of each other."

"The 'bumpiness' of the 'contours of the land'," you say, paraphrasing, "'everything that the consumerist city expelled once it had quickly used it up'–"

"–'battered fridges, yellowing issues of *Life* magazine'–"

"–'fused light-bulbs had accumulated around an enormous junkyard filled with cars'–"

"–'shop windows became covered with cobwebs and mold, lifts in skyscrapers started to creak and groan, posters with advertisements on them turned yellow, egg-holders in fridges filled with chicks as if they were incubators, televisions broadcast whirlwinds of atmospheric storms. The city had consumed itself at a stroke'–"

"–'it was a disposable city following the Moon on its last voyage.'"

"And the people who are marching and the daughters of the Moon all end up on the Brooklyn Bridge," I say. "And –"

"–'the Moon made a last dash, went over the curved grillwork of the bridge, tipped towards the sea, crashed into the water like a brick, and sank downwards'–"

"– and the daughters of the Moon, still attached by ribbons, 'flying over the parapet of the bridge' and arc towards the water and 'disappear amidst the waves'–"

"– and we want to follow them, jump off the Brooklyn Bridge and follow the Moon into the water –"

"– but 'the sea began to vibrate with waves that spread out in a circle,'" you say, "'At the centre of this circle there appeared an island,' 'like a new Moon in the sky.'"

"A new Moon," you say. "And Earth is renewed."

"And 'we gallop across the continent, through the savannahs and forests that had covered over the Earth again'–"

"–'that had covered the Earth again and buried cities and roads, obliterating all trace of everything that had been –'"

"–'and we trumpeted, lifting up to the sky our trunks and our long, thin tusks, shaking the long hair of our croups with the violent anguish that lays hold of all us young mammoths, when we realize that now is when life begins'–"

"–'and yet it is clear that what we desire shall never be ours.'"

The woman with the dark lined eyes is crying.

"It's what the self-appointed leaders of the Whole System Global Education Revolution don't get," I say. "Their arguments are pock marked and pitted with holes, and it's the future lives of our children on Earth that are being gnawed to the bone. Barber says Pearson is building education systems for the leaders of the world in fifty years, but –"

"Montague asked Barber what if Pearson has got it wrong?" you say.

"Pearson *has* got it wrong," I say. "If human societies are to survive, if the human habitability of the Earth is to be sustained, if we are going to do more than gallop across the savannahs, we must change the ways in which we educate children."

"Intuitively, I think parents and teachers know that," you say, eager to move on. "Look," you say, pressing the button on your iPad. "Even though we are not really here, more than the woolly mammoths are left behind."

"All the Tweets, all the YouTube videos, they exist," I say. "There is an extraordinary groundswell that has a solid history of intelligent and informed resistance going back to people like Susan Ohanian[114] who is indomitable. She began blogging after NCLB. Now there are hundreds of bloggers. And then there's Ravitch, whose blog has become a hub for the resistance movement.[115]

"Do you think I could have some coffee?"

"Of course," I say, gesturing to the waiter who doesn't seem a bit surprised that we are still in Café Griensteidl. "I think we have to wrap this up."

"Barber makes bad things sound good," you say. "Like Arne Duncan."

"It's going to be hard," Duncan says, arriving without warning and standing in the middle of Griensteidl between tables 33 and 34. "It's going to be rocky, there is going to be mistakes." Duncan looks confused. "People need to listen, they need to be humble in this and be nimble and make changes. But to sort of stop and go back to the bad old days simply doesn't make sense to me"[116]

The diners stop eating, put down their knives and forks, and stare at Duncan malevolently, as if Macbeth has dropped by for a burger at

Griensteidl.

"Macbeth?" you say. "Not Voldemort? Why did you write Macbeth? The curse!"

"It's hard to not to disrupt the natural order of things," I whisper. "If I think of Duncan Macbeth appears. Shh .We can't interrupt. To us he *is* Voldemort, but to our diners he brings the curse of Macbeth, it's a very serious scene."

"Where is he?"

"Who?"

"Macbeth!"

"Shhh!" the diners hiss in unison.

The woman with black lined eyes at table 24 stands up and looks menacingly at Duncan. She raises an old crabbed hand and points a twisted finger at him. "'The raven himself is hoarse,'" she cries, speaking as Lady Macbeth, "'that croaks the fatal entrance of Duncan under my battlements.'"

"What do *you* want?" Duncan asks, unnerved by the old woman, not knowing if he is Voldemort or Macbeth, but intolerant of insubordination, he attempts to take command of the situation. "'Stay the course'!"[117] he says, repeating himself.

But the diners, whose passion for the theatre is eclipsed by their passion for their children and grandchildren, look at Duncan as if he is the curse of the nation.

"There is 'always lots of drama and noise,'" Duncan says, flat voiced, without thespian flare. "I shouldn't be here."

The old man with the long grey beard at table 24 who looks like Dumbledore stands up, towering over Duncan and making him seem short. "The bad old days?" he says. "They arrived when you appeared."

"This isn't really happening," Duncan says.

"'Of course it is happening,'" the old man says. "'It's happening inside your head, but why on earth should that mean that it is not real?'"[118] [119]

"What's real is that you have taken away children's imaginative play," a woman says, who once played *Mary Poppins* on Broadway and is sitting at table 33.

"Their excitement when they make discoveries," a man shouts out, from table 52.

"Their creative energy."

"*Their minds!*"

"Their passion for justice, for equality," a stagehand from *A Raisin in the Sun* shouts from table 31.

"Their empathy –"

"For one another, for girls and women in society," a woman says who once played Nora in Ibsen's the *Doll's House*, and is sitting at table 14.

"For their mothers and for their teachers—"

"Who you disrespect—"

"For all the attributes that make us human," the woman with black lined eyes says, "that you can't turn into skills, that you can't count at the micron level, that you have taken away from our children, we hold you accountable."

"For the disaster you're inviting," says a man who looks more like the great Shakespearian actor Mark Rylance than Kenneth Branagh, "The weight of calumny is upon you."

By his manner and his guise the diners know he *is* Macbeth.

Unnoticed by the diners, he's been sitting brooding and malevolent at table 3. He is dressed as if he just left the old Globe Theatre more than four hundred years ago. Haggard and dark eyed, he stands, filling Café Griensteidl with old battles that were never won. He walks towards Duncan and speaks directly to him.

"You've raised the anger of this nation's parents and teachers," the man says. "They are greatly offended and for this, the education revolution you've cooked up with Pearson is cursed."

Inexplicably, Duncan, shrunken in stature, lurches one way and then the other, and in his attempt to regain his balance starts turning. No longer in control of mind or matter, he makes three complete circles before, grabbing the back of a chair, he stops rotating. Shaken to his Core, he coughs and spits, uttering a profanity too foul to repeat here.

The mood shifts. Macbeth is gone. Duncan's bizarre behavior breaks the thespian spell and the actors, who until a few moments ago were eating lunch, appear now in their roles as parents and grandparents.

"It's going to be hard," Duncan says, stuck in his own reality. "There is going to be mistakes."

"If my grandson can't make mistakes then neither can you!" says the woman with black lined eyes.

"Our children don't like school!" they tell Duncan.

"Our children have been Pearsonized and demoralized," they say, speaking in one voice.

"They're negative outliers on every social measure when compared with children in thirty other developed nations."[120] [121]

"They're filled with anxiety."

"They get stomach aches more frequently."[122] [123] [124]

"Nightmares and sleepwalking."

"They're hyperactive or suffer from lethargy."

"Cutting is on the rise and some of them talk of suicide."

"They cry a lot."

"And *all* of them bored."

"Bored with the tedium of mechanicky assignments."

"Bored with being trained to use a mouse"

"Bored of practicing drag and drop."

"Bored of learning to fill in bubbles."

"Bored of performing tasks to produce big data that has no scientific validity or reliability."

"Tasks that have been thrown together for irrational reasons."

"That has nothing to do with their ability to actively engage and critically think."

"We are sad that they don't laugh."

"That they no longer have time to play."

Angry about the tedium of their children's lives, and alarmed by how many of their kids have panic attacks when they wake up on Monday morning, the diners begin to shout.

"Duncan, we want you out!"

"It's time for you to go!"

"Duncan's bunkham!" someone shouts.

"Duncan's bunkham! They all chime in.

Until someone shouts, "Send Barber home to Gove! Let the Brits deal with him. Together they've done the UK system in!"

"No more Pearson in our school!" they chant. "Pearson broke the golden rule!"

"No more Pearson in our school!" Louder and louder. "Pearson broke the golden rule!"

"No more Pearson in our school!" Stamping their feet. "Pearson broke the golden rule!"

Then a great bass-baritone from the Metropolitan Opera begins to sing, and several sopranos join in.

"Rule Britannia, no longer rules the waves![125]

"Pearson never, never, ev-er shall be-e- saved!"

Sounding like the chorus in a Gilbert and Sullivan opera, the rest of the diners join in.

"Rule Britannia, no longer rules the waves!

"Pearson never, never, ev-er shall be-e- saved!"

While the chorus is singing Duncan slips away. And you, welcoming his exit, suddenly look alarmed. "Gates!" you exclaim, "Is Gates going to keep funding all this crap?"

"'fraid so," I say, tired and wanting a nap. "It's unlikely any of this would have happened without him."

"Without his money," you say. "Is he coming back?"

"No," I say. "Let's take a different tack." I roll my eyes.

"Is it the rhyming?"

"I'd like not to," I say. "I hope it doesn't put the reader off."

"Not in this piece," you say, picking up your coffee cup and gulping some back. "Come on, Gates!"

"What do you want to know?" Susan Ohanian asks, sitting down in Chomsky's chair. "Gates has been a constant companion of mine. I wrote about him in *Gates of Hell*."[126]

Ohanian is familiar with imaginary friends who have imaginary conversations, and she joins in as if when she grew up her imaginary friends had not gone away.

Once on an outing when she was a child, her sister left her imaginary friend, Nancy, thirty miles away from home, and her uncle, who did not believe in such nonsense, was so concerned about the grieving child he said, "Come on, let's go and get Nancy," and he drove Susan's sister the thirty miles and they found Nancy, and together they all drove home.

"I'll have the Croque Monsieur and frites," she says to the waiter, then smiling at us she adds, "something I wouldn't normally eat" then back at the waiter, " And some roasted mushrooms, since everyone seems to like them."

"We'd better have more coffee," you say,

"Decaffeinated?" the waiter asks, aware of how much coffee we have drunk.

"No, no," you say. "Another espresso, but bring some milk."

"If you want to read about the Gates," Ohanian says, "who bragged that he had 'as much power as the president', and who burst into tears at a Microsoft board meeting, then you need to buy Heilemann's book."[127]

"I dug back before the 1998 Microsoft Antitrust," she continues, as the Croque Monsieur, with Gruyere and béchamel and frites are put in front of her.

"Before 1998," she says, picking up the salt and shaking it vigorously. "Back then Gates didn't have many friends in the media. He was called a bully, the guy with 'the emotional make-up of a petulant 10-year-old', 'egomaniacal and dangerous', and the 'nerd king'."

"But everything changed in 1999 when Gates became the money." Ohanian dips a chip in the ketchup. "In the press Gates became the 'Philanthropist', 'creator of the country's largest charitable foundation', 'the world's richest man', all the descriptors we hear about today."

"Have you read the Glen Ford piece on Gates?"[128] Ohanian asks, as she cuts through the steak. "At *Black Agenda Report*, he has seen the handwriting on the wall for years."

"Ford points out," she says, "'teachers are the biggest obstacle in the way of the corporate educational coup, which is why the billionaires, eagerly assisted by their servants in the Obama administration, have made demonization and eventual destruction of teachers unions their top priority'."

"'Teachers are too damn polite'," Ohanian says, jabbing a frite into the small bowl of ketchup, "'and so, in absence of any real opposition from teachers unions or professional organizations and operating in a fusion of the Marquis de Sade and *The Little Engine That Could*.'"

"That's quite a combination," you say, trying to imagine it.

"Bill Gates has joined up with the US Department of Education," Ohanian continues, "encouraging his pal Arne Duncan to transplant the Microsoft culture of nastiness, frenzied competition, and terror to teachers."

"'And you bet your bippy,'" she says, with another ketchup jab, "'that these folks will speak up for the Gates agenda when the media calls.'" Ohanian eats the frite.

"'There you have it,'" she says. "'You can't quarrel with money. Money is beyond reproach. Never mind that this should be labeled 'vulture philanthropy.'"

"Did you read Gates book, *Road Ahead*?" she asks, not stopping long enough for either of us to say a word. "Dan Kennedy reviewed it.[129] Read the review. Don't bother with the book." She looks at her watch and stands up. "I have to go. It's my afternoon to volunteer at the senior center."

"How do I get out here?" she asks.

"Easy," I say, "but can you stay a little longer?"

"I have a question," you say.

"Be quick," Ohanian says.

"What did Kennedy write in his review of Gates book?"

"That Gates 'spices things up with insensitivity, crypto-fascism, and the numbingly obvious.'" Ohanian says, getting ready to leave.

"What does that mean?" you ask.

"Read the review," Ohanian replies. "Kennedy writes, 'The banality of this isn't that surprising –'," her voice echoes, as if she's left already.

You give me a fierce look and I drink some coffee, and Ohanian impatiently hovers somewhere between here and there.

"–'for Gates, despite his media image, really isn't a technology maven at all," Ohanian says, still quoting Kennedy. She looks down at her see-through self and makes a noise, somewhere between a gasp and an exclamation, and says "transparency!" Then, finishing off the quote from Kennedy, "'Instead, he's a ruthless businessman who got where he is the same way the robber barons of the 19th century did, by buying out or destroying the competition.'"

"Thank you!" you shout. "Take care of yourself!"

"I will!" she says, giving the little laugh that is so characteristic of her.

"Gates," you say again, as if his name is stuck to your tongue and you have to keep repeating it. "We haven't finished with Gates have we?"

I shake my head.

You look at me and I know what you are thinking. Even saying the name of Gates conjures bad luck, and you start spinning, three times round, and spit, uttering an ancient profanity that is unrepeatable here.

A clap of lightening startles us, then thunder, and it starts to rain.

"When the hurly-burly's done," I say, quoting one of Macbeth's witches involuntarily, "when the battle's lost and won."[130]

"That will be'ere the set of sun," you say, looking ancient and ragged.

"Fair is foul and foul is fair," sounding as it will when I am ninety.

"Hover through the fog and filthy air," you say, with an awful stench coming from somewhere.

"Did you spill the ketchup on the table?" I ask.

"It's not ketchup," you say, as you mop up with a tissue you've pulled from your pocket, back to your old self.

"Let's move on," I say. "Do you think this text has been tagged?"

"We might have been, anything is possible," you say, "I think this is paint. But what's the point?"

"*That's* the point, isn't it?" I say. "All tagging does is provide a superficial reckoning of students' performance in relationship to the surface level features of informational texts."

"Totally useless to my teachers," you say.

"What is difficult to understand," I say, "Is that there is no global conspiracy, just a complex set of circumstances that are exacerbated by the madness of a few rich and powerful men."

"Your Voldemorts."

I nod.

"We started with Ferreira."

"A stretch," I say, flattening my hand horizontally and rocking it from side to side. "It's a complement he doesn't actually deserve. He's opportunistic. He'll make a lot of money and cause a lot of problems, but he doesn't come close to Barber, or Murdoch, or Klein, and certainly not Gates."

"You missed out Coleman."

"Ahh, Coleman, Tom Marvolo Riddle, the sincere young man who is actually a Voldemort," I say. "Coleman is self-aggrandizing and opportunistic, an uninformed good speaker who likes to hang out with "data, geeky, cool-people" as he calls them.[131] He's useful to Duncan, Barber and Gates."

"Who's next, Murdoch?"

"An ancient Voldemort," I say. "It's not possible to exaggerate his power. He controls language, not only how it is used, but *how it is learned* in private, for-profit "public" schools. The Governmental hearings in the UK left no doubt that, in the media organizations that he owns, it is language they are after, and he has created a predatory culture in which the cell-phones of murdered children hacked."

"Murdoch himself uses text to injure those who fall foul of him," you say. "He Tweets!"

"Or, has someone Tweet for him," I say. "He kills language by silencing anyone who opposes him, wages war with words, and carries out assaults on democratic discourse through the media outlets he owns. Through News Corp he makes a mockery of the freedom of speech, he makes fools of the opposition, and he shuts down dissent."

"Think of the power of corporations," you say. "They are using tax payer money to subsidize shareholders who are profiting from the privatization of public schools."

"A principal told me the other day," I say, "in New York City the public schools that have not been privatized are now called 'custodial schools'!"

"Madness!"

"When you look at the power of the corporations –,"

" –it's tough for parents and teachers who are protesting the Common Core, or high stakes tests, or school privatization, when the media will not cover their protests," you say. "Last week parents, teachers and principals from New York public schools protested the poor quality of the New York State English Language Arts exams –"

"They protested the poor construction of Pearson tests, which included product placement," you say, "selling products to kids while they were taking the test! And teachers were not allowed to read the test items because to do so is a felony! Parents and teachers protested, but the media didn't cover it. Go figure. But they did cover the pro-privatization of public schools bills in Albany, and then Murdoch –"

"He owns the narrative," I say, nodding. "He's shifted the rhetoric."

"That's it, right?" you say. "He owns the story."

"And he has the power to silence the truth," I say. "Tony Benn, the great British statesman, the great activist in grass roots movements, gave a speech in Bristol in 2006,[132] in which he called Murdoch 'the most powerful person in the world'. Benn said, 'He's got newspapers and television in Australia, here (UK), and America. He's got satellite in

China and these are the people who are really powerful and of course they employ the journalists and control the journalists.'"

"And Barber?" you say, your eyes shining and suddenly you're smiling. You laugh, and people in the restaurant turn and look expectantly –"

"If Barber is Voldemort," you say, loud enough for them to hear, "then Montague is Hermione!"

The laughter follows, a deafening din, and diners stand. Macbeth, Lady Macbeth, Dumbledore, Mary Poppins, and all the parents and grandparents, raise their glasses –

" – A toast" Lady Macbeth says, her voice filling Café Griensteidl. "To Sarah Montague for trouncing the foe!"

"To Sarah Montague for trouncing the foe!" the diners shout. "Barber's out! Pearson has to go!"

"Quick," you say, as the diners take a deep breath, ready to sing "Rule Britannia!"

"Michael Gove!" I say.

"Huh?" you say, as the diners sit.

"Yes Gove," Duncan's British counterpart," I say. "The Right Honorable Michael Gove MP, Member of Parliament and Secretary of State for Education, 'that dreadful man' my mother called him."

"Isn't this getting too complicated?"

"It's complex," I say, "but not complicated. One way or another Murdoch, Klein, Barber, and Gove are all connected. The tragic circumstances that often happen to a child who is Common Cored or Pearsonized are not just isolated occurrences that happen only to one child, or in one classroom, or school, or district, or state, or country."

"I get it," you say. "Like the universe, it's inflationary, spreading like a virus."

"Across the Atlantic, the Pacific. Barber's *'Oceans of Innovation,'*" I say.

"Whole System Global Education Revolution."

"What's happening here, is happening there –"

"And vice versa," I say, "*and* vice versa."

"So when we resist," you say, "we resist for one another. When a parent or a teacher in the US participates in a protest march, she's protesting not only what's happening to her child, to her class, her school, her district, her state, but what's happening to children and teachers on the other side of the pond –"

"You got it," I say. "Pearson's revolution is an attack on children and their parents and teachers –"

"In the US and UK, *and* children in Africa, India, Pakistan – "

"Asia and the Pacific Rim."

"Barber made it clear," you say, "that the world's most vulnerable people create a business opportunity for Pearson. They'll gobble them up and they'll regurgitate them as revenues and profits to their shareholders."

"So it's important that we know about Gove, what he's up to, and the havoc he's wreaking on the UK education system."

"How are we going to do that?" you ask.

"Got your phone?"

"Yes."

"Jess Green," I say, as you enter your code. "Dear Mr. Gove."[133]

And the diners, still listening to the conversation, open a browser. And Jess Green appears, not in person but on their phones. Her Brit voice rings out echoing slightly, the phones not quite in sync, her message reverberating, as the entire restaurant listens to her scold Mr. Gove.

Listening to Green is gut wrenching, tear jerking. She is her own person, loud and brash, and eloquent. She brings the misery of the children and teachers in Brit schools that Gove has revolutionized into Café Griensteidl, and the diners know that what she describes are the lives of US children and teachers that Duncan has ridiculed and trashed.

"I am seeing things from your side," Jess Green says, "and honestly I sympathize –".

" –But now try seeing them from mine –"

" –The sun is going down, leaving the school in darkness and we are going home, passing cars carrying passengers that are going home for the day, can put their work out their heads, open a bottle, talk to their partners, and we sit marking –"

" –You just try doing this seven days a week, eighteen hours a day, yes and at the weekend when we are not teaching with the workload it feels much the same –"

" –And if after forty years of this you want to take my pension away, leaving me no option but to carry on till I'm seventy-eighty, when I barely know my own name, and eventually I drop dead in front of class 7a. Well Mr. Gove even if I am the only one on this picket line, I will be the one standing in your way."

"United we opt-out," you say, as the diners clap, shout "bravo", wipe away their tears, and shake their heads.

"Gove has led an unprecedented attack on the teaching profession and continuously denigrates one of the hardest working set of people in the country," a teacher writes, in response to an article on Gove in *The Guardian*. "Every teacher I know is in school by half past seven, leaves at 6 and then does a couple of hours of paperwork when they get home. Every teacher I know cares passionately about the children in their care."

"Gove is definitely a Voldemort," I say, "and so is Dominic Cummings, who was Gove's special advisor. Cummings was educated at Oxford and fits right in with the entitled Etonian chums who run the Brit government. They all suffer from elitism and exceptionalism."

"So if Cummings has been ousted, why is he important?" you ask.

"Because he left behind him a 250 page document[134] that has got a lot of attention from the press in the UK[135] because of his statements on intelligence and genetics."

"It's only a matter of time," you say, looking troubled, "before –" then changing tack, "have you read it?"

I nod.

"And?"

"He's supposed to be a genius. A Brit boffin."

"What?

"An egg-head. A brain."

"And?"

"One of my friends is a psychiatrist who had a patient who was educated at Harvard," I say. "A brilliant man who was paranoid schizophrenic and kept insisting that he had written a treatise of national importance. My friend asked me if I would read it."

"Well?" you say, sounding impatient "was it?"

"I shake my head."

"And Cummings?"

"He's taken some brilliant and some not-so-brilliant research and made it rubbish," I say. "It's a pseudo-intellectual rant, a mock treatise, long quotes, one after another, and strings of disorganized ideas that obfuscate the breaks in Cummings' thinking."

"Is he mad?"

I shrug. "Not my field –"

"As an academic," I say, "what concerns me is that the paper is filled with ideas that are not his own but that he includes without reference – "

"He's a plagiarist?"

"Not exactly," I say. "He's not quoting without reference. But he does take credit for the scientific work of others, especially the research of

Earth systems scientists, which he most certainly is not –"

"He also misrepresents the work of eminent scientists, and uses their research for his own peculiar purposes –"

"Example?"

"The distinguished biologist E. O. Wilson on '*Consilience*',"[136] I say. "He quotes Wilson a lot. He has an "if-Wilson- said -it, -it -must -be -so" attitude".

"So what's—"

"Consilience? Jerry Fodor in the *London Review of Books* calls it an 'epistemological thesis'"[137]

"You're losing me."

"That's the point," I say. "Cummings is showing off. It's like he is sneering. 'I'm –smarter- than- you- are', actually, 'I'm- a- genius- and –you're- not' –"

"It's mad," I say. "It's bad. And, it's brilliant."[138] [139]

"Get back to Fodor," you say, shaking your head.

"Fodor writes that consilience 'roughly' means 'all knowledge reduces to basic science' and that this kind of epistemological physicalism cannot account for the metaphysical'— "

"Ahhgh! Translate! –"

"It means Wilson left out a lot of important ideas" I say, "Fodor calls Wilson's book 'a shambles'. He writes that Wilson's use of 'recidivist Associationism with engineering jargon' is depressing."

"Is it?"

"'fraid so," I say. "What's interesting is that Fodor, in his review of Wilson's book dismantles one of the key points that Cummings makes in his rubbishy piece. It's the one that's at the center of the Whole System Global Education Revolution that Barber and Pearson are in the process of marketing, and that Gove in the UK and Duncan in the US are forcing on children and their teachers."

"You're losing your reader!" you say, giving me the time-out hand sign, "can we skip this bit?"

"Let's take it just a little bit further," I say. "This is more than a game that we are playing. Fodor unravels the underlying scientific argument of Cummings, Gove, Duncan, Barber, Coleman, Ferreira, Klein and Murdoch, actually Murdoch doesn't have a scientific argument, but Gates does, so *and* Gates! It's very exciting!"

"Okay," you say. "But be quick, before readers start turning off their electronic devices or turn the page of their paper copies!"

"Will you just listen?" I say. "I'll make it quick. Fodor provides a scientific rationale for our imaginary conversation. Back at the beginning –"

"God that seems a long time ago!"

"Ferreira said, 'everything in education is correlated to everything else.' Right? 'And every single concept is correlated in a predictable way to everything else using psychometrics' and you said he was 'dangerously naïve' and that's how we got into this imaginary conversation in the first place."

"Consilience?"

"That's it," I say. "He talked of producing lots of data at the 'granular level'.

'As if that gives the data scientific legitimacy," you say.

"Exactly," I say.

"And how does Fodor counter that?"

"Fodor argues, and I'm leaving a lot out, that 'events fall into revealing and reliable patterns not just at the level of microstructure –'"

"Ferreira's 'granular level' –'"

"Right," I say. "'Not just at the level of microstructure, but at many different orders of aggregation of matter'—"

"So," you say. "The argument that Fodor makes undermines the whole assessment system for the Common Core, rocks the foundation of Pearson's Whole System Global Education Revolution, and does away with the rationale for companies like Knewton."

"Yes!" I say. "It's all based on a faulty scientific premise!"

"No scientific validity?"

"None!"

"'The heterogeneity of our discourse,' Fodor reasons, corresponds to the 'heterogeneity of levels at which the world is organised, and both might well prove irreducible'. He names different kinds of physical things."

"Some are protons," Fodor says, "some are constellations, some are trees or cats, some are butchers, bakers, or candlesticks."

"Not candlestick makers?"

"No, candlesticks." I say. "Think about the lists we can generate from our imaginary conversation! Physical and metaphysical, trans-disciplinary, drawing on philosophy, on the social sciences, and on literature – in all forms from novels and short stories to drama and poetry, and framing it all in the political moments of our time –"

"And mythological, and mystical and magical!" you say. "Don't forget culinary!"

"That's funny," I say. "Fodor recommends the antipasti."

"What?"

"He writes, 'The talk about nodes, linkages, long-term banks and resonating circuits is entirely meretricious and adds nothing but the show of connections with the computational sciences', which he says Wilson has misunderstood. Then he states, "If this is what consilience is like, I recommend the assorted antipasti!"

"And silly and foolish, and based on sound reasoning, but back-up," you say, looking serious. "There is a counter list. "Do you honestly believe that just because the CCSSO, NCTQ, edTPA, PARCC, are all based on faulty science that the madness will stop? That Pearson, the College Board, Wireless Generation, America's Promise Alliance, Student Achievement Partners, the Council on Foreign Relations, McKinsey &Co., many of which received mega-funding from Gates, will care a toss that the education initiatives of their corporations and non-profits are based on crap science?"

"No, I'm not expecting that," I say. "But it's important that parents and teachers know that the architects of the Whole System Global Education Revolution have no hold on science. It's important," I say, repeating myself, convinced this is a matter of great urgency, "that they know the scientific basis of the militaristic attack on human systems of language and thought is dangerously reframing people's life on the planet is fatally flawed."

"I think we have to stop being nice," you say. "At the risk of sounding crass, it doesn't take a feminist to notice the organizers of the Whole System Global Education Revolution are rich white men. There I said it. You can't write about silencing and stay silent."

"Let's start with where the leaders of the coup d'état and where they went to university. Everybody knows Gates went to Harvard. Who else?"

"Duncan – Harvard."

"Klein – Columbia and Harvard."

"Ferreira – Harvard,"

"I think of Ferreira as a derivative trader."

"Still Harvard."

"Barber – Oxford."

"Murdoch – Oxford"

"Coleman – Oxford and Cambridge."

"Gove – Oxford"

"Cummings – Oxford."

"No one from CUNY? No state university?" you ask.

I shake my head.

"No degrees in multicultural education. No teaching certifications. No degrees in child development. No expertise in language development or the development of reading and writing. No training in science. No physicists. No biologists. No Earth system scientists. No doctorates in any related field."

"Not likely!" I say. "Our Voldemorts who went to Oxford are enculturated into unreflective, arrogant, elitist, imperialistic, Anglo-centricity."

"You're getting verbose. Why not just 'Upper class'?" you say. "The ruling elite of the global empire on which the sun never sets."

"The dominions," I say. "The colonies, the protectorates, and the territories, so vast that when the sun is setting in one dominion it is rising in another."

"And now instead of colonizing countries," you say, "they are colonizing our schools and the minds of our children, here in the US as well as the UK. And Africa, *and* India, *and* Pakistan, *and* Asia *and* the Pacific Rim, *including* Australia."

"For he is an English man!" our bass-baritone from the MET at table 23 stands up and sings, and the diners in Café Griensteidl, the sopranos and tenors, stand and sing the Gilbert and Sullivan song with him.[140]

"He is an Englishman!

For he himself has said it

And it's greatly to his credit

That he is an Englishman!"

"Rule Britannia, no longer rules the waves!" sings one of the sopranos, who has a son in third grade and a daughter in eighth grade.

"Pearson never, never, ever shall be-e- saved!" the diners join in.

A woman sitting at table 53 gets up who has not spoken before. She has greying dark brown hair cut straight just below her chin and a fringe that would be called bangs here. She is wearing a loose silk blouse, in pale peachy pink, and navy blue baggy trousers so her form is carefully concealed. She puts her hands in her pockets and walks deliberately around the room, as if the diners are in grammar (high) school.

The diners have no problem being in her class. They know that the woman is Dorothy Lintott in *The History Boys* by Alan Bennett[141], and she is preparing a class of senior boys for their interviews for Oxford and Cambridge University. Dorothy is the only woman in the classroom and Irwin, another teacher, is coaching the boys on lying at their interview. A third teacher is present.

Hector, a large recumbent diner sitting at table 43, who looks as if he would have difficulty if he had to stand, speaks as if Irwin is in the room. He says, loud enough for all to hear, "May I make a suggestion? Why can they not all tell the truth?" Then skipping some lines that Irwin would say, he looks from his repose and smiles at Dorothy, gesturing with his arm, hand open and flat – her cue.

" I hesitate to mention this, lest it occasion a sophisticated groan, but it may not have crossed your minds that one of the dons who interviews you may be a woman," Dorothy says, walking around Café Griensteidl looking at the diners in their worldly sophistication, and seeing nothing more than eighteen year olds who long to be sophisticated. "I'm reluctant at this stage in the game to expose you to new ideas, but having taught you all history on a strictly non-gender-oriented basis I just wonder whether it occurs to any of you how dispiriting this can be?"

A diner at sitting at table 12 yawns on cue. Dorothy frowns at him.

"It's obviously dispiriting to you, Dakin, or you wouldn't be yawning."

"Sorry, miss," the diner says.

"Women so seldom get a turn for a start," Dorothy says, as she walks from table to table, desk to desk. She looks at a diner who knows he is Timms, and skipping lines she says, "Am I embarrassing you?"

"A bit miss."

"Why?"

"It's not our fault, miss. It's just the way it is."

There is some talk of Wittgenstein, and Dorothy takes her hands out of her pockets, and placing them firmly on her hips she turns full circle looking at the boys at their desks and the diners at their tables.

"Can you, for one moment," she asks, her voice bitter but not broken, "imagine how dispiriting it is to teach five centuries of masculine ineptitude?" Her voice rises, "Why do you think there are no women historians on TV?"

In Bennett's play there are comments on female anatomy, and protests from Hector, who shouts "Hit that boy!" that Dorothy leaves out, as she gets to the critical moment in her performance.

"I'll tell you why there are no women historians on TV, it's because they don't get carried away for a start, and they don't come bouncing up to you with every new historical notion they've come up with –" she pauses, stares at one of the diners, "the bow-wow school of history."

She stares at another diner then turns and addresses everyone in Café Griensteidl as if they were her class.

"History's not such a frolic for women as it is for men. Why should it be? They never get round the conference table. In 1919, for instance, they just arranged the flowers then gracefully retired." Dorothy's hands are back in her pockets. She speaks as one who has endured a lifetime of misogyny.

"History is a commentary on the various and continuing incapabilities of men."

There are murmurs around room from the women diners who don't have roles in the play. Their anger is rising, and they root for Dorothy and mouth the words as she speaks.

"What is history?" Dorothy asks, looking from one boy to another. "History is women following behind with the bucket."

"And I am not asking you to espouse this point of view but the occasional nod in its direction can do you know harm"

Silence. The diners know that this is a moment in the play when nobody speaks. The wait staff stand still, including the servers, and the maître d'.

"You should note, boys, that your masters find this undisguised expression of feeling distasteful, as, I see, do some of you."

The diners are clapping, holding up their glasses.

"To Dorothy! Bravo!"

"I read a letter in the *London Review of Books* a few years back," I say, "written by a man who had gone to a grammar school. He said when he arrived at Oxford another new student told him he was the first "grammar school boy" he'd ever met. You know Barber, Gove, and Cummings all went to private schools."

You give me the hand sign for a time-out.

"Do you realize how many ideas you've let loose? Class, gender, race, prejudice and discrimination, elitism and fanaticism, not to mention child abuse and a global coup?"

"They're not separate categories," I say, "and they are all constitutive characteristics of the coup."

"I know they are endemic, but –"

"When nine white men from Oxford and Harvard align themselves in such a way that they have the power to aggressively pursue a Whole System Global Education Revolution, then every discriminatory practice that is humanly possible comes into play, requiring acts of resistance, of consciousness raising, and of confronting ourselves and our passive acquiescence to their tyranny."

"It's overwhelming," you say.

"Only if we let it be," I say. "You've read Pierre Bourdieu."

You nod and smile. "If you have I have too!"

"Bourdieu writes of Anglo-American ideology and of the super rich and those condemned to poverty."

"In *Acts of Resistance*[142] Bourdieu states, 'A large part of social suffering stems from the poverty of people's relationship to the education system, which not only shapes social destinies but also the image they have of their destiny – ', which, he goes on to state, 'undoubtedly helps to explain what is called the passivity of the dominated, the difficulty in mobilizing them, etc.'"

"I think what you are saying is that if we are *to act* we have *to know* the history of the men who have instigated the coup?"

"That's it," I say. "Bourdieu refers to Max Weber, who said that 'dominant groups always need a theodicy of their own privilege.'"

"He could be writing about privileged white men," you say, "who are educated at Oxford and think their very existence justifies a global coup in education."

"Bourdieu qualifies Weber's theodicy and calls it 'more precisely, a sociodicy,'" I say. "He writes, 'in other words a theoretical justification of the fact that they are privileged.'"

"But how do we get that across in an imaginary conversation?" you ask. "There are great sociological tomes written about this."

"Let's have another skit."[143]

The diners clap, ready for an elaborate game of charades, to expose the forces at work that silence the poor, both women and men, and make their children weak.

"I know my place!" the diners shout, banging their hands on the table, "I know my place!" They are looking at table 9 at which Gates, Murdoch, Klein and Barber sat. The man sitting there slides off the bench seat and slowly stands up. It's John Cleese the celebrated Brit actor and comedienne, of Monty Python and Fawlty Towers. He is very tall and thin, taller still when he puts on a bowler hat. He picks up a long black umbrella and taking exaggerated strides, he makes his way to the middle of Café Griensteidl and stands, looking down his nose, perfectly still.

"I know my place!" the diners shout, as another man, of shorter stature and much larger in girth, dining by the window at table 20, pushes back his chair, stands, and puts on a trilby hat. His name is Ronnie Barker, another Brit actor who often performs with Cleese. He walks to the middle of Café Griensteidl and stands next to the very tall man with the umbrella and bowler hat.

The din is deafening. Phones are out. Diners are videoing.

A small man rushes out of the kitchen untying a white apron, and someone gives him an old jacket with a zipper that he puts on and leaves undone, a woolly scarf, and an old cloth cap. His name is Ronnie Corbett, the third Brit and comedian in the 1960's skit revived for the occasion of this imaginary conversation.

Corbett in his cloth cap stands next to Barker in his trilby hat, and Barker stands next to Cleese in his bowler hat. The three men are in a line, very tall and thin, shorter and tubby, and little and puny. In a similar way to their hats, their relative size indicates their positioning in British society. They are all looking straight ahead.

"I look down on him," Cleese says, turning his head and looking down at Barker, "because I am upper class."

Cleese turns and looks forward as Barker turns his head and looks up at Cleese.

"I look up to him because he is upper class," Barker says. He turns and looks down at Corbett, "but I look down on him because he is lower class."

"I am middle class," Barker says, looking straight ahead.

Not a sound.

Corbett is still looking straight in front of him. He carries the line in a by quiet deferential way, that no italic or bold text can match.

"I know my place."

Laughter fills Café Griensteidl.

Corbett turns and looks up at Barker and Cleese. "I look up to them both. But I don't look up to him" he indicates Barker with the slightest gesture of his body. Then speaking emphatically, "But I don't look up to him," again the gesture indicating Barker, followed by standing on his toes and a gesture at Cleese, "as much as I look up to him, because he has got innate breeding."

Corbett faces front.

Pause. Laughter. Quiet.

"I have got innate breeding, but I have not got any money." Cleese bends at the knees. "So sometimes I look up to him." As Cleese drops down, Barker grows taller that Cleese by standing on his toes.

Cleese stands up facing forward.

"I still look up to him," Barker says, now flat footed and looking up at Cleese again. "Because although I have money, I am vulgar." He turns his head and looks down at Corbett. "But I am not as vulgar as him. So I still look down on him."

Barker looks forward.

Pause.

Coffee cups are halfway up.

"I know my place," Corbett says.

The din is deafening, people are laughing and some coffee is spilt. Corbett, Barker and Cleese wave as they fade. Soon just a few diners are left.

"How's it going to end?" you ask.

"The conversation or the coup?"

"Both I suppose."

"It's a mystery," I say, smiling, and then more seriously, "My granddad was a little man like Corbett. Dug coal underground until he was seventy. My other granddad was a miner. Digging coal killed him. He dropped dead when he was fifty. Before I was born."

"My father went down the mines at fourteen and joined the army at the beginning of the Second World War, when he was twenty four. He spent six years in North Africa. Came home and worked at Dunlop's stoking the furnaces to make car tires. In 1950 he joined the RSPCA and we moved to Ashford in Kent. I was three.

"Lady Richie, who was one of the patrons of the Royal Society, came to the house that we'd been given just after we'd moved in. My mother introduced me by my Welsh name. Lady Richie, whose daughters were called Fiona and Louise, told my mother my name was too long for a little girl."

"Call her Denny," she said.

"My mother bent her knees, not quite a curtsy, and bowed her head in a silent, 'Yes, your majesty'. When my father came home she told him that Lady Richie had changed my name. I remember their perplexed faces looking down at me. They never called me by my real name again."

"The first time I realized Lady Richie had no right to take away my name, I was at Columbia University studying for a doctorate. In a seminar on language and identity we were asked to share how we got our names. It was the distress of the other students when I told my story that, quite frankly, surprised me."

"It wasn't that I was anaesthetized. Miners were lower working class. I knew my place and I rejected it. I watched as my friends crossed off the days, then weeks, on calendars that they kept in their desks, tearing off the X'd-out months until the term when they were fifteen. They knew their place even if I didn't."

"Rebellion for me was getting an education, holding on with my fingers nails when the ladder was pushed out from under me. When I was fifteen when I got nine O-levels at the secondary modern, and on my first morning at grammar school and the new students in the sixth form lined up after assembly to meet the Headmaster, I stumbled when he told me to spell my name and he told me university was "not for the likes of me."

"I have a photo of Lady Richie and Sir James, giving my dad an award for bravery from the Royal Society of Prevention of Cruelty to Animals. He got a lot of awards and I don't know which one it was. She looks so elegant and refined in the photograph, regal, like the Queen. I never questioned her sense of entitlement. It was, of course, a manifestation of a deeply rooted and pernicious form of cultural pathology, and my unquestioning acceptance of my name being changed is also a form of cultural pathology."

"Hegemony isn't just an abstract idea," you say. "It's Cleese, Barker, and Corbett."

"It's Denalene," I say. "That's my name."

"The point you're making is that this is a particularly pernicious form of cultural pathology that's gone viral," you say. "And the hosts, who're carrying the infection, are some rich and powerful men, all educated at Oxford –"

"And Harvard –"

You nod. "All of whom seem to think it's their innate right to change the way we educate our children, in the same way Lady Richie thought she had the innate right to change your name."

"That's about it!" I say. "I was worried for a minute that I'd lost the point, but that's it, exactly."

"There's no such thing as 'innate breeding' that privileging entitlements," you say, "the hierarchical social structures that are exemplified by 'I know my place', can only exist when there's a cultural pact between those who patronize and those who are patronized."

"Yes!" I say. "Tear up the pact. Reject the agreement. But we still have to figure out how to do that."

"Sounds like an ending coming up," you say. "Is there anything we haven't covered? That you don't want to leave out? Before we get the end?"

I hesitate. "Something about Cummings, and something about Gates."

"Let's start with Cummings," you say. "Are you sure he's not insane?"

"Honestly I have no idea. From reports in the Brit press his behavior was a problem. A woman staffer who had been at the Department for Education for twenty-seven years is reported in *The Independent* newspaper to have formally complained about 'a macho culture of intimidation, favoritism and 'laddism' at the DfE.'[144] The article states that she singled out Cummings stating that he was 'widely known to use obscene and intimidating language."

"Obnoxious if not mad," you say.

"You could say that," I say, "I have no idea. Nevertheless, the deconstruction of his writing does raise concerns about the state of his mind. He's thrown a hand grenade or more accurately, dropped a bomb."

"Go on."

"Genetics," I say. "In that rubbish paper he writes about intelligence, wealth, and character, and genetic explanations of variance," I say. "He also writes disparagingly about 'gender differences' and with almost Arian discrimination, about the 'selection of elites."

"History repeats," you say.

"Cummings says it seems very accurate to him that the existence of McKinsey, BCG and Bain is due to the difference between 'genuinely intelligent and talented 'creators' and the mediocrity of the average Ruler."

"I'm not getting it," you say. "Are you trying to tell me the take away from Cummings piece is that rulers are mediocre so McKinsey a.k.a. Pearson are the real source of power in the world and they tell the rulers what to do?"

"It's the we're smart-your-leaders-are-stupid rationale for Pearson's Whole System Global Education Revolution," I say.

"Okay," you say, nodding, expecting more.

"'There is strong resistance,' Cummings writes, 'across the political spectrum to accepting scientific evidence on genetics. Most of those that now dominate discussions on issues such as social mobility entirely ignore genetics and therefore their arguments are at best misleading and often worthless.' Cummings claims research shows that as much as 70% of a child's performance is genetically derived."

You are shaking your head.

"The problem is that even though there's gobs of research to refute what Cummings has written, the press in the UK[145] picked up on what he said," I say. "*The Guardian* headline questions whether he is a 'genius or a menace', and writes that he is 'arguably the most brilliant and most controversial special advisor in the coalition', *and*, give me strength! Such cods-wallop! 'His 250-page screed sprawls across a vast canvas about the future, education, Britain's place in the world and disruptive forces ahead.'"

"If he's left the government to start the equivalent of a charter school does it matter?" you ask, smiling even though you drop your head in your hands, "of course it matters."

"He's put the idea that genetics counts back on the agenda," I say, "and predictably it's been picked up by the media. The headline in Brit *Mail Online* was 'Genetics outweighs teaching: Michael Gove's right hand man says it is IQ, not education, which determines child's future.'"

"And you're saying that what Cummings wrote has negative consequences here in the US," you say.

"That he's profligating dangerous ideas, that have no scientific legitimacy –"

"And," you say, determined to finish your sentence, "he's leaving out areas of research that are critical to our understanding of the education of our children and the future of humanity."

"You've got it. The issues have become obfuscated in the UK," I say, agreeing, "but inherent in Brit culture is the common understanding that the upper class are smarter than the middle class and the middle class are smarter than the lower classes."

"The upper class go to Eaton and run the country," you say, "the upper middle classes run the corporations, the lower middle classes become clerks and functionaries, and the lower classes are left begging."

"Do you remember Alan Sokal wrote a paper in which he deliberately made stuff up?" I ask. "It was called "Transgressing the Boundaries: Towards a Transformative Hermeneutics of Quantum Gravity".[146]

"The article was published in *Social Texts* in the summer edition of 1996."

"And Sokal revealed that the article was a hoax in another article that he published in *Lingua Franca*, that same summer," you say.[147]

"The difference is that Sokal 'fessed up," I say. "His purpose was to open up a conversation about science, about intellectual imposters, about modesty, rigor, and irony, and about knowledge in and of the world."

"And you think Cummings is an intellectual imposter?"

"He is," I say. "He leaves out whole chunks of science. For him genetics and IQ are still fixed. *The Mismeasure of Man*, Stephen Jay Gould called it.[148] He would get a better grip if he read *The Practices of Human Genetics* that Everett Mendelsohn edited."[149]

You make the cut sign with your hand, and I nod, knowing it's time to end the conversation but not quite willing to let it go.

"Cummings doesn't get systemic complexity. His piece isn't even a parody. In all likelihood he couldn't write one. He isn't a genius. He's an imposter, incapable of modesty, rigor, or irony. Nevertheless, his ideas lie between the lines of Barber's *Oceans* piece."

"And by extension," you say, "like Cummings' paper, the Whole System Global Education Revolution is founded on an elaborate hoax."

"I would say so," I say.

"And Gates?"

"None of this would be happening without his money," I say. "But here's the kicker. Some of the big data men are using their electronic contraptions to quite literally penetrate children's minds, and Gates is paying. *Affective Computing* they call it. They are experimenting with the ways they can hook children up to computers to measure their biological responses to computerized tasks."[150]

"That's hard to believe," you say. "Don't you think the government would put a stop to it?"

"The government is participating," I say. "Arne Duncan is on board."

"The purpose of some of the research, which Gates is funding, is to penetrate children's minds to measure blood flow et cetera and to track their emotional response to the tasks they are made to do," I explain. "You can go to the source and read about it on the US Department of Education website. I regard the plans for *Affective Computing*, as the mind molestation of children on a national scale."

"Can it get any worse?" you ask. "Are you sure Gates is funding it?"

"He is," I say, "'physiological response data from a biofeedback apparatus that measures blood volume, pulse, and galvanic skin response to examine student frustration in an online learning environment.'"

You give me the right hand on top of the fingers of the left hand time out.

"You're giving me another time out now?" I say. "I thought you wanted to finish."

"Listen to me!" you whisper. "When governments and corporations start entering the minds of people all bets will be off!"

"How do you know it is not already taking place?" I ask. "This situation is Earth shattering. Even the contemplation of experimentation on children in the US is enough for a step change in human life on the planet."

"What happens here ricochets around the world," you say. "At this time in human history the dangers are incalculable!"

"Why do you think we are having this conversation?" I whisper back. "Isn't that exactly what we have been taking about?"

"Is everything okay?" our waiter asks. "More coffee?"

"Espresso," you say, adding. "We're just leaving."

"Yes," I say.

"Doubles," the waiter says, hurrying off.

"Before we go on," I say, still whispering. "Have you read CIOMS's *International Ethical Guidelines for Biomedical Research Involving Human Research?*"[151]

"Give me strength!" you say, rolling your eyes. "CIOMS?[152] No. Why?"

"Council for International Organizations of Medical Sciences."

"I'm convinced after studying the CIOMS *International Ethical Guidelines for Biomedical Research Involving Human Subjects* that the governmental policy makers and the corporate and philanthropic sponsors of the revolutionary changes that are taking place in K-12 public education are in violation of the international agreement," I say. "The guidelines include both medical and behavioral studies pertaining to human health. There's irrefutable evidence that the new mandates are negatively affecting the health and wellbeing of students, and this affective computing is unquestionably bio-medical, physical, chemical, and psychological."

"What are the critical guidelines that are being violated?"

"That participants are capable of deliberation about their personal choices," I say.

"That they have choices," you say. "Self-determination."

"Children don't," I say. "And neither do their parents or teachers."

"What else?"

"The rights of vulnerable persons must be protected."

"And they are not."

"No," I say. "Irrefutable fact. Children who are terminally ill are being made to take the tests. A brother and sister whose parents were killed just before the mandated tests in April were denied exemption. Children who are struggling with profound disabilities aren't exempt."

"They write whatever they know," you say. "One child who had to take the fifth grade test is reading on a first grade level. But he still had to take the test. He did his best. He wrote every word he knows. One child wrote passages from the bible that he had memorized. Others wrote expletives all over the test. One child just wrote his name, over and over again."

"Do no harm," I say. "There's substantial evidence that children are being harmed by the developmentally inappropriate curricular changes that are taking place."

"CIOMS? What else?"

"The agreement of each child has been obtained to the extent of the child's capabilities," I continue, "and a child's refusal to participate of continue in the research is respected."

You nod.

"The well-being of the human subject should take precedence over the interests of science and society," I continue.

"Do no harm," you say. "Nonmaleficence."

"Which includes safeguarding confidentiality," I say. "Secure safeguards of all data."

"Have such safeguards been put in place?"

"To the contrary," I say. "We can safely say the data on children has already been sold to the highest bidder."

"We've gotta be vigilant," you say. "Look for signs, look for cracks. We'll find them in the language when they appear."

"And be aware of the perils of obedience," you says.

"Stanley Milgram and his electric shock experiments," I say, "and the dilemma of inherent submission to authority, published in *Harper's Magazine* in 1973."[153]

The waiter arrives and puts two glasses of brandy on the table.

"We didn't order any brandies," you say.

"Complements of the maître d'," the waiter says, as he puts the espressos next to the brandies and grins. "It's not every day both Bill Gates and Noam Chomsky, and all the others come to Café Griensteidl," he says, adding, "not to mention Macbeth –"

The waiter's eyes go unnaturally wide. You grab the empty tray as he begins to turn, spinning three times before he stops and spits and utters an expletive that is particularly gross. Offering profuse apologies, he grabs one of the brandies, drinks it in one gulp and chases it down with the other.

"We're running out of time," you say.

"It's important that people know about the experiments on *Affective Computing* are supposed to increase the grit, tenacity, and perseverance of children living in poverty," I say.

"When racial and ethnic minorities are disproportionately represented," you say. "It's a whole other conversation we've all gotta have."

"What's clear from this and other analyses is the Whole System Global Education Revolution *is* a destructive coup that jeopardizes the future of Earth and Earth's children."

There is a moment of quiet and you say, "go on" and I smile shaking my head.

"It's tough," I say. "We can't leave this very real imaginary conversation without talking about what's happening to women."

"Mothers and daughters."

"We've had the stuffing knocked out of us."

"Annihilated."

"Or, plasticized and laminated."

"You've been watching *Fox*!" you say, laughing.

I shake my head. "I've been rereading Adrienne Rich, *On Lies, Secrets, and Silences*,"[154] I say. "What is clear from the Whole System Global

Education Revolution is that the very rich and powerful men who have instigated the coup are aggressively using force to overtly threaten and manipulate children's caregivers, their mothers and teachers."

"Predominantly women," you say.

"It's a gendered struggle," I nod, "in which some men are supportive of women, while some women have reaped the benefits of aligning themselves with the dominant masculine apparatus of the privatization of public education."

"What complicates it," you say, "is that this is a class struggle as well as a gendered struggle."

"I know my place," I say, and we both laugh.

"No you don't!"

"My place," I say, "is to 'rail against the exclusion of women from learning and power', as Adrienne Rich does when she quotes Virginia Wolf who writes in *Three Guineas*[155] 'Where in short is it leading us, the procession of the sons of educated men.'"

"Rich points out that Wolf is writing about the connections between war and fascism and patriarchal systems of governance," you say.

"The idea that we're preparing our children for armed conflict is already out of the bag. The *Council on Foreign Relations*, which is a private think tank, produced the heinous *US Education Reform and National Security Report*.[156] Klein co-authored the report with Condoleezza Rice. Barber was an advisor. Gates provided financial support. It's another infamous document that supports the privateers' public school grab and the imposition of the corporate Common Core to prepare US children for war.

*In which twelve venerable women scholars with more than
500 years of teaching experience refuse to capitulate to the
demands made by nine rich men who have no teaching
qualifications or teaching experience*

ACT FOUR

"Do you remember what Adrienne Rich writes about witches?"

"'The witch persecutions of the fourteenth through seventeenth centuries' –"

"Who said that?" you ask, looking around Café Griensteidl.

"' – between the illiterate but practiced female healer and the beginnings of an aristocratic nouveau science, between the powerful patriarchal Church and enormous numbers of peasant women' –"

"Some women have gathered where Gates, Murdoch, Klein, and Barber were sitting," I say.

The speaker continues and we get up and go listen.

"' – between the pragmatic experience of the wise woman and the superstitious practices of the early male medical profession'–"

"It's Adrienne Rich," you whisper. "Her memory in your mind."

"' – The phenomena of woman-fear and woman-hatred illuminated by those centuries of genocide are with us still.'"

The women who are with Rich have pulled the tables together, and we stand with other women who have gathered around the ones who are sitting at the tables. They all seem oblivious to our presence; so intense is their conversation.

Standing with us is the woman with black lined eyes who was Lady Macbeth. She has her arm around the shoulders of the woman who was Dorothy Lintott in *The History Boys*. The man with the long grey beard who played Dumbledore is on the other side of the woman with black lined eyes, and he is holding her hand. I am next to Dumbledore. The woman who played Nora in Ibsen's *A Doll's House*[157] is standing next to you, squeezed in next to a woman who looks remarkably like Sarah Montague.

Other women, mothers and teachers, have come into Café Griensteidl with the intent of confronting Barber with their phones to video and Tweet, but finding he has long gone they have made their way to where the women are sitting. Their cell phones are in their hands and they are already uploading to YouTube and sending Tweets.

Susan Ohanian is back. Morna McDermott,[158] the great organizer is here. Leonie Haimson[159] who routed inBloom. Jess Green the Brit poet comes back and men of the resistance also appear. Daniel Ferguson after taking on Coleman. Anthony Cody, who is writing *The Educator And The Oligarch* as we speak.[160] Rick Meyer, who in gentle and peaceful ways, spends every moment working with teachers and organizing. And Pablo Muriel, whose empathetic pedagogy and scholarship carries forward the compassion and caring of the great progressive educators of the 20th century.

The women at the tables 50 and 51 are deep in conversation.

"'In no culture more than in Western Culture is the failure of ideas like 'industrialization' and 'development' more evident," Adrienne Rich is saying, "' – and with the apparent 'freedom' of unveiled and literate women, the condition of woman has remained that of a nonadult, a person whose exploitation – physical, economic, or psychic – is accepted *no matter to what class she belongs.*'" [161]

"I don't know all the women sitting at table?" you whisper with some urgency.

"They're some of the women I read," I whisper back. "I was thinking about them. It was not my intention to bring them here. They just appeared."

A woman standing next to me whispers "Hush!"

"Do you realize there are nine women?" you ask, doing no more than mouth the words.

"Purely by chance," I whisper, as the woman I don't know, hisses "Shhhhh!"

Five are sitting on the bench seats against the wall with the big mirrors behind them, and four are on the other side of the table facing the mirrors, so their faces can easily be seen by the listeners to the conversation.

"You'd better name them."

"Adrienne Rich is in the far corner," I say. "Next to her is Simone Weil, of *Gravity and Grace.*"

You nod.

"Hannah Arendt, *The Life of the Mind* and *The Human Condition,*[162] is sitting next to Simone Weil."

"And Toni Morrison, *Jazz*[163] and *Beloved,*[164] is sitting next to Hannah Arendt."

"She's also here for her Nobel Speech, which those nine rich and powerful men should copy out five hundred times –"[165]

"And recite each day before breakfast!" you say.

"Maxine Greene is next to Toni Morrison. Have you heard Maxine speak about *Jazz* and *Beloved*? It's a forever memory," I say. Greene's *Releasing the Imagination* is a remarkable book. I once heard her say she wished she had written it with a pencil because she wanted to write more about the dark side of imagination."

"Who's at the end on the other side of the table sitting opposite Rich?"

you ask.

"Virginia Woolf," I say. "*Three Guineas* and *A Room of One's Own*.[166] Listen ... she's saying something about education."

"The questions that we have to ask and to answer," Virginia Woolf says, speaking with unhurried clarity, "about that procession during this moment of transition are so important that they may well change the lives of men and women forever."

Virginia Wolf pauses and looks at the gathering of women, as if she expected to be at the table. Her words carrying her forth.

"For we have to ask ourselves, here and now, do we wish to join that procession, or don't we? On what terms shall we join that procession? Above all, where is it leading us, the procession of educated men?"

"Let us never cease from thinking," Virginia Woolf continues, "what is this 'civilisation' in which we find ourselves? What are these ceremonies and why should we take part in them? What are these professions and why should we make money out of them?" And again she asks, "Where in short is it leading us, the procession of the sons of educated men?"

"The technicians are ignorant of the theoretical basis of the knowledge which they employ," Simone Weil says, speaking quietly but in a clear voice that everyone can hear.

"In how many countless and unconscious ways do we capitulate to the demand for numbers?" the woman says who is sitting next to Virginia Woolf.

"Is that Mina Shaughnessy?" you ask. "*Errors and Expectations*?"[167]

I nod. "Let's listen. She's talking about big data and teaching."

"In how many ways has the need for numbers forced us to violate the language itself," Mina Shaughnessy asks, "ripping it from the web of discourse in order to count those things that can be caught in the net of numbers?"

"In the last analysis," Hannah Arendt says, "confirmation of any scientist's theory comes about through sense evidence." She adds, "This is true even of the most complicated mechanical instruments, which are designed to catch what is hidden from the naked eye."

"The recognition of human wretchedness is difficult for whoever is rich and powerful," Simone Weil says, "because he is almost invincibly led to believe that he is something. It is equally difficult for the man in miserable circumstances because he is almost invincibly led to believe the rich and powerful man is something."

"An ever-increasing progress in wealth," Arendt responds, "can only assume even more radical proportions if it is permitted to follow its own inherent law."

The people standing around the tables seem to be increasing, some are making videos others Tweeting, many are just watching and listening.

"Wealth accumulation as we know it is only possible if the world and the very worldliness of man are sacrificed," Hannah Arendt says.

"The process of production and consumption", she says –

" – is central to the Whole System Global Education Revolution," I whisper to you –

" – the expropriation of people and world alienation coincide *and collide*", Hannah Arendt says, before turning to "the role of language in struggles for human existence."

"Analogies, metaphors, and emblems are the threads by which the mind holds on to the world," she says, "even when, absentmindedly, it has lost direct contact with it, and they guarantee the unity of experience."

"Maya Angelou is sitting next to Mina Shaughnessy," you whisper. "*I Know Why the Caged Bird Sings* and *Phenomenal Woman*."

"She's telling the women seated at the table how the authors and illustrators of children's books came to write the letter to President Obama.

"We wrote," Maya Angelou says, as she did at the beginning of this conversation, "to express our concern for our readers, their parents and teachers. We are alarmed at the negative impact of excessive school testing mandates including your Administrations own initiatives, on children's love of reading and literature."

"Our public schools," Maya Angelou says, putting her hands flat on the table, "spend far too much time preparing for reading tests and too little time curling up with books that fire their imaginations."

"This is a historic moment," you whisper, "this conjuring of brilliant minds, a sharing of the lightness of being as well as the dark side of imagination."

"Together," I whisper back, "without knowing what the future will bring, they are rewriting their narratives, creating a dialogic, co-joining their own personal stories and wisdom with the stories and wisdom of everyone who reads what they are saying."

"Just being on this page," you whisper, "in this imaginary conversation, we are reclaiming our lives and our work as activists and advocates. Re-inventing ourselves as teachers and scholars. We are exploring the ethical stances that we take, our philosophical beliefs, and pedagogical practices."

"Listen," I whisper, "Toni Morrison is telling everyone that the future of language is in our hands."

"The vitality of language lies in its ability to limn the actual, imagined and possible lives of its speakers, readers, writers," Toni Morrison says. "They know that 'it arcs toward the place where meaning may lie.'"

"Be it grand or slender," she continues, "burrowing, blasting or refusing to sanctify: whether it laughs out loud or is a cry without an alphabet, the choice word or the chosen silence, unmolested language surges toward knowledge, not destruction."

There is a quiet moment. The women at the table know that their own ways of knowing are not recognized, and they speak, as Rich writes in "When We Dead Awaken: Writing as Re-Vision,"[168] about the "misnaming and thwarting" of women's needs by "a culture controlled by males" and of the "problems of language and style", and the problems of "energy and survival."

"Sometimes we do not survive," you whisper with tears in your eyes, knowing you will be gone soon, and that there are women at the table who lost their lives in the struggle to survive.

"I think Adrienne is talking about Anne Sexton," you say, "and the read-in she organized at Harvard against the Vietnam War."[169]

"Famous male poets and novelists were there," Adrienne Rich says, "reading their diatribes against McNamara, their napalm poems, their ego poetry." She pauses. There is a clatter of dishes from the kitchen, but other than that total silence.

"Anne read," Adrienne Rich says, "in a very quiet, vulnerable voice." She names the poems. "Little Girl, My String Bean, My Lovely Woman."[170]

"She set," she says, "the first-hand image of a mother's affirmation of her daughter against the second-hand images of death and violence hurled that evening by men who had never seen a bombed village."

"Anne was forty-five when she committed suicide," you say out loud, and the women at the table look at you, and your color rises, as they sadly smile.

"We die," Toni Morrison says, quoting from her Nobel speech, "That may be the meaning of life. But we do language. That may be the measure of our lives."

"Every woman who writes is a survivor," Adrienne Rich says, quietly reaching out for the hand of Virginia Woolf, who walked into the Ouse River close to her home with stones in her pockets.

"Every woman who is a mother and teacher is also a survivor," Morna McDermott says, receiving nods from the women at the table and from those who are standing listening to the conversation.

There is another pause in the conversation that is also written in the silences that seem naturally to occur. Maxine Greene picks up the thread. She speaks of Virginia Woolf and her consciousness of "moments of being".

"She knew," Maxine Greene says, looking at Virginia Woolf as if they often sit together and talk, "how rare they are in any given day and how necessary for the development of a sense of potency, of vital being in the world."[171]

Maxine Greene talks extemporaneously of breaking "the bonds of the ordinary and the taken-for-granted" and moving "into spaces never known before", and of wanting this "for those who teach."[172]

"Some of you know enough about me to know that I feel that I'm never finished," Maxine says, "I can't finish if things are always incomplete." She speaks of talking with the teaching artists at Lincoln Center about the uses of the arts in a dark time. "These artists want to know what use art is in a time like this, and without being optimistic, or using perfect prose, or sentimentality, we have to find things that connect us, through a variety of languages, not only verbal language, but dance and music."

There is a murmur in the room, a low resonant sound, of confirmation and affirmation from the diners in the arts who have gathered around.

"It's worthwhile to empower teachers," Maxine Greene says, "and in turn, their children, to speak in a way that they feel names their worlds, that allows them to use their imagination, to move beyond, to move toward the possible, and today."

"I still feel the incompleteness involved," Maxine Greene says. "I have to think it through as I always do. I've never asked the questions I've been asking with quite the feeling that I am asking them now. What use are they? What use is this? How do I create myself as someone who can somehow be of help?" Maxine looks around the table, "I think we're all thinking about that."

Louise Rosenblatt, *Literature as Exploration*,[173] is also at the table.

"This conversation seems to grow in significance as the minutes pass," Louise Rosenblatt says. "Those who sit back and wait are, I believe, ignoring the children whose lives will be affected," Louise writes. "To minimize the bad effects on good schools as well as the poor ones, we must try to influence what is happening. If we fail, as well we may, we shall at least have spread the ideas, have educated some who will continue the resistance."[174]

"It really has to be a mutual admiration society that we're in here at the table," Louise Rosenblatt continues, smiling at Maxine, "because we've all been in this so long together and we've certainly, in one way or another, been working towards the same goals, and that's the important thing to keep in mind."[175]

"Maxine took a course that Louise taught when she was studying for a doctorate," I whisper. "Maxine knew Dewey and Louise knew Ruth Benedict and Franz Boaz and she shared a room at Barnard with Margaret Mead."

"How old was Louise when she spoke the words she is speaking here in today?"

"She was ninety seven," I whisper. "She lived to be one hundred and one."

The women around the table say words that celebrate Louise's life, and in that celebration they recognize their own. Those who are standing around the table clap and laugh and enjoy the moment when belonging to this community of great teachers, and listening to them speak validates their struggle to teach.

"And one of the things I've always been fighting is stereotypes," Louise says, speaking louder above the din, "and one of the stereotypes is the idea that when you're ninety you're done for, but I'm not in my dotage yet."

Again there is laugher.

"I went to college in nineteen twenty-one," Louise says, "Women got the vote in nineteen twenty!"

Their joyfulness fills Café Griensteidl, and just for a moment "their conversation is like a gently wicked dance," as Toni Morrison writes in *The Bluest Eye*,[176] "sound meets sound, curtsies, shimmies, and retires. Another sound enters but is upstaged by still another," as the women at the table "circle each other and stop. Sometimes their words move in soft spirals; other times they take strident leaps, and all of it is punctuated with warm-pulsed laughter – like the throb of a heart made of jelly."

"We didn't have many books," Louise Rosenblatt says, "but there were books, books that were important to me because my father talked to me about them. In those days, the Darwinian idea of 'survival of the fittest' was being used to justify unbridled economic competition. The government accepted no responsibility for the inequality of opportunities for the individual."

"She could be talking about today," you whisper.

"When workers joined in unions, employers could hire thugs to attack them. I can remember hearing about such events," Louise says.

"Like today," someone says, and others standing around the table agree.

"Kropotkin's *Mutual Aid*,[177] presented a different view of evolution," Louise says.

"There was also cooperation. There was care and fidelity among animals as well as human beings. For me, to think about, to make meaningful, an idea such as mutual aid was very important. I acquired the belief that, no matter what your gender, your race, your religion, everyone was entitled to life, liberty, and the pursuit of happiness that did not harm others."

"Having lived through all the wars of the last century," Louise says, "I have seen repeatedly how defense of democracy from threats from without can foster threats from within to our civil liberties and our democratic way of peaceful change and improvement. That's why I am worried about this situation we are in now."

"Ninety-seven years are difficult to fit into such a short period of time," Louise says, wanting to continue talking but knowing that others have not had a turn to speak. She ends by saying that through almost all of the ten decades of her life, the humanitarian love of democracy has been her inspiration, and it is this inspiration that fills the room.

Around the table the women are quiet.

"There is a lot that the UK and US can learn from the woman of Africa," a woman says, as she sits down next to Louise Rosenblatt and introduces herself to the other women at the table.

"That's Wangari Maathai," I say. "She was the first African woman to receive the Nobel Peace Prize.[178]

"Ten!" you say. "There are ten women now!"

"Sometimes the conversation has a mind if its own," I say, raising my shoulders in an exaggerated shrug.

"The Nobel Committee said, 'She thinks globally and acts locally,'" you say, "and that is exactly what we must do."

"There is a need to galvanize civil society and grassroots movements to catalyse change," Wangari says. "I call upon governments to recognize the role of these social movements in building a critical mass of responsible citizens, who help maintain checks and balances in society. On their part, civil society should embrace not only their rights but also their responsibilities."

"Further, industry and global institutions must appreciate that ensuring economic justice, equity and ecological integrity are of greater value than profits at any cost," Wangari says. "The extreme global inequities and prevailing consumption patterns continue at the expense of the environment and peaceful co-existence. The choice is ours."

"Throughout Africa," Wangari says, "women are the primary caretakers, holding significant responsibility for tilling the land and feeding their families."

"The women we worked with recounted that unlike in the past, they were unable to meet their basic needs," Wangari says, "and I came to understand that when the environment is destroyed, plundered or mismanaged, we undermine our quality of life and that of future generations."

"Tree planting became a natural choice to address some of the initial basic needs identified by women," Wangari continues, "So, together, we have planted over 30 million trees that provide fuel, food, shelter, and income to support their children's education and household needs."

"Initially, the work was difficult because historically our people have been persuaded to believe that because they are poor, they lack not only capital, but also knowledge and skills to address their challenges," Wangari says, "Instead they are conditioned to believe that solutions to their problems must come from 'outside.'"

"In order to assist communities to understand these linkages, we developed a citizen education program, during which people identify their problems, the causes and possible solutions," Wangari says. "They then make connections between their own personal actions and the problems they witness in the environment and in society."

"They learn that our world is confronted with a litany of woes: corruption, violence against women and children, disruption and breakdown of families, and disintegration of cultures and communities."

"I would like to call on young people to commit themselves to activities that contribute toward achieving their long-term dreams," Wangari says. "They have the energy and creativity to shape a sustainable future. To the young people I say, you are a gift to your communities and indeed the world. You are our hope and our future."

"Kids have needs," Yetta Goodman says, as some of the teachers who are listening to the conversation push tables 52 and 53 together with tables 50 and 51 so all the illustrious scholars can sit together.

Yetta slide in on the bench seat.

"Eleven!" you say.

"We need her," I say with a smile and shrug. "She's one of the greatest educators of our time."

"Wait!" you whisper, as another very old woman who is looking down, slides in beside her.

"Twelve! Who's that beside her?"

"I can't see her face," I whisper.

"You brought her here!"

I shake my head.

"How did she get here then?"

"Yetta," I say. "Yetta must have been thinking about her."

"Are you saying Yetta's brought her own imaginary friend?"

I nod.

"But –"

"Be quiet!" the woman next to me says in a loud voice.

"Shhhh!!" The people standing around the table hush her.

"It's Emilia Ferreiro!" I say, catching a glimpse of her face. "Yetta and Emilia are great friends."

Yetta smiles at Emilia.

"It is my great pleasure to introduce to you Emilia Ferreiro," Yetta Goodman says. "Emilia's discoveries have had an important influence on our work and the work of scholars around the globe."[179] She pauses.

"We are concerned that her conclusions and insights built on a highly respectable research tradition have not been part of recent discussions about reading instruction taking place at the federal level."

"The recent focus on literacy in the United States," Yetta continues, "has used narrow research findings to mandate the use of skills and commercial reading programs appropriate for classroom use."

"At a time when reading research and instruction are often reduced to test scores, Emilia's significant contributions about how children learn must be highly visible and in the mainstream of our current debates."

"Emilia was born in Argentina and completed her dissertation under the direction of Jean Piaget," Yetta says. "Her research is published in Spanish, English, French, Italian, and Portuguese. All of her research reflects her concerns for social justice, linguistic self-determination, socio-cultural issues and democracy, as well as her belief that literacy and biliteracy are human rights."

"Among her many honors," Yetta says, smiling at Emilia, "she has received is the Libertador da Humanidade medal from the state of Bahia in Brazil, previously awarded to only two well known personalities, Nelson Mandela and Paulo Freire."

Emilia is small and her grey hair is in a long braid that rests on one shoulder and hangs down in front of her. The way she speaks makes it quite clear she is a woman of great intellect and determination.

"My role as a researcher," Emilia Ferreiro says, after greetings to the women at the table, "has been to show and prove that children think about writing, and that their thinking demonstrates interest, coherence, value and extraordinary educational potential."[180]

"We've got to listen to them," Emilia says, emphatically, "from the very first written babbling," she says, "from the moment they made their first drawing."

"We cannot reduce children to a pair of eyes that see," she says, "a pair of ears that listen, a vocal mechanism that emits sounds and a hand that clumsily squeezes a pencil and move it across a sheet of paper."

"Behind or beyond the eyes, ears, vocal chords and hand lies a person who thinks and attempts to incorporate into his or her own knowledge, this marvelous medium of representing and recreating language which is writing, all writing."

"Los niños tienen la mala costumbre de no pedir permiso para empezar a aprender," Emilia says.

"Children have the bad habit," Yetta translates, "of not asking for permission *to begin* learning."

"Los niños," Yetta says, using her arms, hands facing up, to invite everyone to repeat the incantation.

"Los niños tienen la mala costumbre de no pedir permiso para empezar a aprender."

Emilia smiles and gestures for Yetta to speak.

Yetta picks up the thread. She talks about the progressive educators with whom she studied. She traces her own history, and her life-long dedication to the study of language and how children learn to read and write, back to John Dewey and his concept of the "power of experience".[181]

"I knew that's the kind of teacher I wanted to be," she says.

" – and I walked into classrooms where I was encouraged to be a progressive educator. I know a lot of you think that the resistance is just now and just new, but this was the early fifties, and we thought it was new then too."

"I learned later," she says, "that it was going on fifty years earlier in the 1900's in other places."

She talks about Bank Street School of Education and Lucy Sprague Mitchell.

"Teachers were working in similar ways," she says, "and so I began to be immersed in the idea of letting kids discover knowledge, getting kids involved in all kinds of experiences."

"Kids want to use literacy for important purposes," she says, "and for the emotional realm of our humanness."[182]

"These are issues to understand and to ponder and to disseminate," Yetta says, inviting conversation as she always does.

She turns to those of us standing and listening, and creates a public space to discuss what is happening to children in public schools, to teachers, to families, and to the planet, because of the obsessions and fetishes of self-aggrandizing rich and powerful men.

"We cannot let circumstances incapacitate us," a young teacher says.

"We are, *not yet*," another declares, smiling at Maxine Greene, who often has been heard to say, "I am, not yet."

"We have to resist," another says. "We have the right to name ourselves."

"Teaching is an intellectual act," the first teacher says. "But it's also a political act.

"When we name ourselves as teachers we do so with compassion, with caring, and with intellectual integrity."

"What's important are the relationships teachers and students have with each other."

" – build community –"

" – trust –"

" – participate in projects –"

" – solve problems for the public good –"

" – social inequality –"

" – what's happening to the planet –"

" – be prepared for emergencies –"

" – live in the world together –"

"So!" Yetta Goodman says. "Where do we go from here?

Yetta stands up.

"I want to talk about what we need to do together," she says, "with parents, teachers, and concerned citizens to change what is happening in public education."

Yetta's voice grows louder.

"We need to demand that government and policy groups act on the basis of the best knowledge," she says, growing taller and getting louder.

Yetta begins to rap.

Teachers hold up their cell phones. They video. They Tweet.

"We must support classroom teachers as they resist harmful mandates," Yetta says, louder and much taller than a few moments ago.

"Los niños tienen la mala costumbre de no pedir permiso para empezar a aprender," we all rap back.

Yetta's rapping gets louder. Her voice can be heard outside on 72nd where Broadway meets Amsterdam.

People stop and look around to find out where the speakers are located. Dog walkers are in motion and babies in buggies bop to the beat.

"We need to help parents support teachers," Yetta says, "who know how to involve their students in authentic literacy experiences, as they inquire in excited ways about their learning discoveries."

Horns honk. Trucks stop. Car windows open. Drivers clap as Yetta raps. The traffic jams. Young people with samplers, sequencers, and drum machines, arrive on the scene. They have synthesizers, and turntables. Keyboards, Motif and Phantom, are quickly set up.

A producer appears and puts an old record on an MPC and samples the drums, then keeps it on a replay loop, then chops it up, making a new sound, as people holding coffee cups dance around.

And in Café Griensteidl, Yetta continues to rap and the great women at the table begin to clap.

"We can partner with parents to influence politicians concerning decisions."

"Los niños tienen la mala costumbre de no pedir permiso para empezar a aprender,"

Yetta raps about curriculum and testing and the few people left sitting in Café Griensteidl jump up.

"We must challenge policy makers to consider knowledge over political agendas," Yetta raps.

"Los niños tienen la mala costumbre de no pedir permiso para empezar a aprender," we rap back.

Yetta raps about political decision-making. She is taller than Duncan. Richer than Gates. Cleverer than Barber. More eloquent than Coleman. More syncopated than Beyoncé.

"How do we and many, many, many, more," Yetta raps, "stand up and shout, 'Hell no!' and get the word out!"[183]

On the street people shout, "Hell no! Get the word out!"

Food vendors and face painters appear, and children laugh and shout and jump about.

"Bill Gates does not have our consent, to use our kids in his experiments!" a mother shouts.

"Hell no!" the crowd shouts. "Get the word out!

"What do we say when Pearson tries to test our kids?" another mother shouts.

"Hell no! Get the word out!"

"What do we say when they take out schools?" she shouts.

"Hell no! Get the word out!"

"Free our schools!" a father shouts. "Free our kids! The Common Core is on the skids!"

"Free our schools!" the crowd shouts. "Free our kids! The Common Core is on the skids!"

"Everything important is worth doing carefully," Louis C.K. tweets. "None of this feels careful to me."[184]

"Why should school be so hard," Diane Ravitch writes on her blog, "that it makes children cry?"[185]

"Free our schools! People rap. "Free our kids! The Common Core is on the skids!"

"Stop the rot!" parents shout. "Public school is all we've got!"

Inside Café Griensteidl everyone joins in, including the great women.

Adrienne and Simone, Hannah, Toni and Maxine, Wangari and Louise, Maya, Mina, Virginia, and Emilia, stand up and clap as Yetta raps, and you know what I am thinking.

"You are thinking about your own life, I know."

"Our histories unite us," I say, "our collective experience."

"Slavery, the Pogroms, and the Holocaust."

"Dirty Wars, World Wars, and Diasporas."

"Past and present," you say.

"We have experienced the rape of our countries."

"We know first-hand the suffering of huge movements of displaced people forced to leave their homes to flee violence and oppression."

"Across class lines, we know what it is like to be discriminated against –"

" –because of our gender, our religion, out ethnicity, and our race –"

" –rape, physical abuse, and mutilation –"

"No *Chariots of Fire* in green and pleasant lands," you say.[186]

"Some of us have hid when there were tanks in the street, stood with our hands up, guns pointed at us –"

" – 'but still, like dust, our spirits rise,'"[187] you say, quoting Maya Angelou.

"We know first hand the triumph of the human spirit," I say. "The lightness of being, and life's deadly weight."

"Our lives are testimony to the imaginative possibilities of women's talents and strengths."

"Our endurance," I say.

"Our capacity to say "hell no!"

"Our struggle for human dignity and self-worth is not just for ourselves," I say, "but for the collective good, and for the good of our children –"

" – their *right to childhood* – "

" – unencumbered by an oligarch's damaging experiments –"

" – or colonized by some titled peer from the UK with dominion desires fulfilled through a global education revolution."

"Let us *not* praise famous men,"[188] [189] we say, knowing that it doesn't matter who's speaking.

"Children have a right to a *free and public education*," I say. "For the pursuit of human knowledge and understanding that is *free* of corporate greed."

"We should not have to ask permission," you say, "for teachers to teach in developmentally appropriate ways that inspire and excite, and enhance our children's incredible capacity to learn – "

" – for the sheer joyfulness of their lives and for their lightness of being."

And around the table, this coven or council of great women, agree.

"We are and always will be," they say together, "defenders of every child's right to a childhood free of despots and demons, except those they imagine when playing with friends."

"In solidarity!"

There is a moment of laughter and hugs around the table as one by one the great women begin to fade … until only Emilia and Yetta are left. They are much smaller now, their voices no more than a whisper. They smile at the teachers, hold out their hands to them, and together they are gone.

"Time to go," I say, as the wait-staff separate the tables, cover them with white table cloths and put place settings on them ready for dinner.

"Wait!" you say. "Is it the beginning of the end, or is something else beginning?"

"It depends," I say.

"On what?"

"On whether we stand up tall like Yetta? Emilia? The twelve women?"

"And?"

"Dump Pearson," I say.

"You're not serious!"

"Barber and Pearson are taking our children in the wrong direction," I say. "His Whole System Global Education Revolution is a global social catastrophe, a total system failure."

"So what can we do against such recklessness?"

"The madness will stop if we refuse to participate," I say. "The struggle for democracy is always ground up."

"Remember Watson in the House of Commons inquiry into Murdoch's business practices?" I add. "We have cowered before them long enough'. We have the capacity to create humane social learning environments for children. For the common good. For our kids. If we don't stop the madness, we're jeopardizing their future."

"And we're culpable as well," you say. "And Gates?"

"Make it a crime for oligarchs to interfere with democratic social systems," I say. "It's vote tampering on a national scale."

"He's violating the rights of fifty million children. Jeopardizing their future," you say. "Send him to jail."

"Tell Gates we choose decency and democracy and not the *in*decency of his oligarchy. He does *not* have the power to dictate how our children are taught in public schools."

"Tell him we refuse to participate in his Common Core experiments," you say. "Ban the use of galvanic skin devices in affective computing trials that he's funded."

"Tell him to stop wasting his money. To spend it for the Common Good," I say. "Build new public schools. Create parks in poor urban neighborhoods. Make sure there are health centers. Medical care for everyone in the community."

"Tell him to put his money into Earth friendly low-income housing."

"Libraries. Media centers."

"Work with local leaders. Make sure they're not exploited."

"Habitat for Humanity."

"Create opportunities for the mothers and father of children who are poor to find employment in urban renewal projects in their own communities."

"And young people."

"And plant lots of trees for Wangari Maathai. Gates could learn a lot from her."

"Pearson could too," I say. "Tell Barber we take back our independence. That US public schools are no longer under Pearson's colonial rule."

"Support a United Opt-Out day," you say.

"A national Opt-Out Earth friendly day," I say. "A day of re-imagining *public* education."

"Not an imaginary opt-out day," you say, frowning at me, and we both laugh.

"No," I say. "A real re-imagining. A re-visioning. A day in which parents and teachers make public schools anew."

"Where children love learning," you say, "and teachers are given the freedom to create opportunities for children to become intellectually capable young people with the creative minds, healthy bodies, and ethical spirits that they need to contribute wisdom, compassion, and leadership in a global society, which is the mission of Lakeview where Gates's children go to school."

"'To become creative, independent people,'" I say, "as Chomsky says, 'who can find excitement in discovery and creation and creativity at whatever level or in whatever domain their interests carry them.'"

"Draw on the wisdom of great teachers," you say. "Women *and* men."

"Paulo Freire is of critical importance," I say.

"We should be asking 'what is Mahatma Gandhi's position on education?'" you say. "Nelson Mandela's?"

"What our venerable women and these very great men have in common is that they don't separate scholarship from human experience," I say. "Their students' lives are not separated from their academic learning –"

" – becoming literate is more than learning to read and write, it is becoming critically conscious of what is happening to us in the world –"

" – *and* what is happening to the world – "

" – the great threats to people and the planet"

"It's why teachers are silenced," I say.

"And gagged."

"What is demanded of them is passivity and acquiescence."

"What gets me is the utter stupidity of it," you say. "Teachers are bullied. Threatened. Forced to carry out irrational mandates. Then when their stupid policies don't work, they blame teachers, when it's the teachers who suffer the incompetence of misguided rich and powerful men."

"It's misogynous," I say. "The majority of teachers are women. We're fooling ourselves if we think they are not being persecuted today. Many teachers live in fear –"

" – including the men who teach with them"

"They're frightened for themselves, for their families, and the children they teach. Their wretchedness is not recognized. Because of this children are suffering."

"It's a fourteenth century witch hunt," you say. "Between the great knowledge and pragmatic experience of wise teachers. Most of whom are women. And the superstitious practices of rich and powerful men who know little, have not taught, and are so pumped up with their own importance it makes me sick!"

Adrienne Rich," I say, nodding. "The phenomena of woman-fear and woman-hatred illuminated by those centuries of genocide are with us still."[190]

"Teachers are endangered," you say. "Soon a whole generation of wise women and great teachers will be extinct."

"I *am* extinct," I say. "My generation of teachers is fading away. Our only hope for young teachers, both women and men, is that we stay long enough to end the Whole System Global Education Revolution instigated by a few contemptible delusional men."

"And make it a new day," you say.

"Oh, I wish ..." I say. "I wish for parents and teachers and especially children, a kind and caring world, and a *very* new day."

"Make Earth a child safe zone," you say, smiling at me as you go.

"Let's hope so," I say, as I fade away.

Erased.

REFERENCES

1. Postman, N. (1982), *The Disappearance of Childhood*. New York, NY: Delacorte Press.

2. Montaigne, M de. (1579). *Of the education of children*, in *The Complete Essays of Montaigne, Book 1 (26)*. Stanford, CA: Stanford University Press (1958).

3. Mars-Jones, A. (2014, May 8). More Pain, Better Sentences. *London Review of Books, (36)*9, 27-30. Retrieved from http://www.lrb.co.uk/v36/n09/adam-mars-jones/more-pain-better-sentences

4. Taylor, D. (2014, forthcoming). *Keys To The Future: A Teacher's Guide To Making Earth A Child Safe Zone*. New York, NY: Garn Press.

5. "...oozing droplets of topaz-colored sweat", from Calvino, I. (1968). *The Daughters of the Moon*.

6. Calvino, I. (1968). *The Daughters of the Moon*. In *The Complete Cosmicomics*. UK: Penguin Classics (2009). Also published in *The New Yorker*. (2009, February 23). Retrieved from http://www.newyorker.com/fiction/features/2009/02/23/090223fi_fiction_calvino

7. Shakespeare, W. (1623). *Macbeth*.

8. "Is this the end?" I ask mechanically, with no idea what I mean."Or the beginning," she says, without moving her lips."What do you mean?" I ask. "It's the beginning of the end, or something else is beginning?"Adapted From Calvino, I. (1968). *The Daughters of the Moon*.

9. Collins, S. (2008). *The Hunger Games (Book 1)*. New York, NY: Scholastic Press.

10. Rowling, J.K. (1998). *Harry Potter and the Sorcerer's Stone*. New York, NY: Scholastic.

11. Dahl, R. (1964). *Charlie and the Chocolate Factory*. New York, NY: Alfred A Knopf.

12. Ferreira, J. (2012, October 9). Presentation at the U.S. Department of Education *Education Datapalooza: Unleashing the Power of Open Data to Help Students, Parents, and Teachers*. Retrieved from https://www.youtube.com/playlist?list=PLhdwy3ASoEfm1QeH0kfNnLWUqv4lE1pPs *or* https://www.youtube.com/watch?v=Lr7Z7ysDluQ&list=PLhdwy3ASoEfm1QeH0kfNnLWUqv4lE1pPs&index=19

13. Bakhtin, M. (1975). *The Dialogic Imagination*. Austin, TX: University of Texas Press (1981).

14. Arendt, H. (1978). *The Life of the Mind*. San Diego, CA: Harcourt Brace Jovanovich.

15. Greene, M. (1995). *Releasing the Imagination*. San Francisco, CA: Jossey-Bass.

16. Ferguson, D.E. (Winter 2013-2014). Martin Luther King Jr. and the Common Core: A critical reading of "close reading". *Rethinking Schools*, 28(2). Retrieved from: http://www.rethinkingschools.org/archive/28_02/28_02_ferguson.shtml

17. Coleman, D. (2012, December 5). Presentation video on the *engageNY*, New

York State Education Department website. Retrieved from http://www.engageny.org/resource/middle-school-ela-curriculum-video-close-reading-of-a-text-mlk-letter-from-birmingham-jail

18. King, M.L. (1963, April 16). *Letter from Birmingham Jail*. Retrieved from: http://www.stanford.edu/group/King/frequentdocs/birmingham.pdf *or* http://www.uscrossier.org/pullias/wp-content/uploads/2012/06/king.pdf

19. New York State Education Department. (2011, April 28). *Bringing the Common Core to Life: Introduction to the Common Core State Standards for English Language Arts & Literacy*. Video presentation by David Coleman (Part 4). Retrieved from http://usny.nysed.gov/rttt/resources/bringing-the-common-core-to-life.html *or* excerpt at https://www.youtube.com/watch?v=Pu6lin88YXU

20. New York State Education Department (2011, April 28). *"Bringing the Common Core to Life": David Coleman. Founder, Student Achievement Partners*. Transcript of presentation retrieved from http://usny.nysed.gov/rttt/docs/bringingthecommoncoretolife/fulltranscript.pdf

21. Ada, A.F., Alexander, A., Ancona, J., Angelou, M., et al. (2013, October 21). *Public Letter on Standardized Testing from Authors and Illustrators of Books for Children and Youth*. Retrieved from: http://www.fairtest.org/public-letter-on-standardized-testing-by-childrens-authors

22. Morpurgo, M. (1982). *War Horse*. New York, NY: Scholastic Press.

23. Pullman, P. (1995). *The Golden Compass: His Dark Materials (Book 1)*. New York, NY: Alfred A Knopf.

24. Angelou, M. (1995). *Phenomenal Woman: Four Poems Celebrating Women*. New York, NY: Random House.

25. Angelou, M. (1970). *I Know Why the Caged Bird Sings*. New York, NY: Random House.

26. King, M.L., Jr. (1963, August 28). *I Have A Dream*. Retrieved from http://www.youtube.com/watch?v=smEqnnklfYs

27. King, M.L., Jr. (1963, August 28). *I Have A Dream*. Retrieved from: http://www.archives.gov/press/exhibits/dream-speech.pdf

28. *Future Earth*: http://www.futureearth.info/

29. Planet Under Pressure 2012 Conference, London, England, March 26-29, 2012. *New Knowledge Towards Solutions.* http://www.planetunderpressure2012.net/

30. Field, C.B., Barros, R.B., et al (2014, March 31). *Summary for Policymakers: Climate Change 2014: Impacts, Adaptation, and Vulnerability*. Contribution of Working Group II to the Fifth Assessment Report of the Intergovernmental Panel on Climate Change (IPCC). Retrieved from http://www.ipcc-wg2.gov/AR5/

31. Boonstra, W.J., and de Boer, F. (2014). The Historical Dynamics of Social–Ecological Traps. *AMBIO, 43*(3), 260-274. Retrieved from http://link.springer.com/article/10.1007/s13280-013-0419-1 doi:10.1007/s13280-013-0419-1

32. Taylor, D. (2014). *Nineteen Clues: Great Transformations Can Be Achieved Through Collective Action*. New York, NY: Garn Press.

33. *Goldfinger* (1964). Third movie in the *James Bond* series based on the book

Goldfinger by Ian Fleming (1959).

34. Chomsky, N. (2012, February 8). *Education For Whom and For What?* Presentation at the University of Arizona. Retrieved from https://www.youtube.com/watch?v=e_EgdShO1K8

35. *United Opt Out*: http://unitedoptout.com/

36. *Badass Teacher Association*: http://www.badassteacher.org/

37. *Save Our Schools*: http://saveourschoolsmarch.org/

38. Leonie Haimson, *Class Size Matters*: http://www.classsizematters.org/

39. Susan Ohanian: http://www.susanohanian.org/

40. Potsdam Memorandum 2007 - A Global Contract for the Great Transformation. *Symposium on Global Sustainability: A Nobel Cause*, Potsdam, Germany, October 8-10, 2007. Retrieved from http://www.nobel-cause.de/potsdam-2007

41. Brito, L. & Stafford Smith, M. (March 29, 2012). *State of the Planet Declaration*. Planet Under Pressure 2012 Conference. London, England, March 26-29, 2012. Retrieved from http://www.planetunderpressure2012.net/

42. Gee, J.P. (2013). *The Anti-Education Era: Creating Smarter Students through Digital Learning*. New York, NY: Palgrave Macmillan.

43. Gee, J.P. (2013, August 27). Personal email communication.

44. Taylor, D. (1998). *Beginning to Read and the Spin Doctors of Science*. Urbana, IL: National Council of Teachers of English.

45. 105th US Congress. (1998). H.R. 2614, *Reading Excellence Act*. Retrieved from http://www.gpo.gov/fdsys/pkg/BILLS-105hr2614eh/pdf/BILLS-105hr2614eh.pdf

46. 107th US Congress (2002, January 8). Public Law 107-110, *No Child Left Behind Act of 2001*. Retrieved from http://www2.ed.gov/policy/elsec/leg/esea02/index.html or http://www2.ed.gov/policy/elsec/leg/esea02/107-110.pdf

47. Cambourne, B. (2012). *Seven Conditions of Learning*. Adapted from Cambourne, B. (1988). *The Whole Story: Natural Learning and the Acquisition of Literacy in the Classroom*. New York, NY: Scholastic. Slides downloaded from http://www.slideserve.com/torie/cambourne-s-seven-conditions-of-learning

48. Cambourne, B. (1995). Toward an educationally relevant theory of literacy learning: Twenty years of inquiry. *Reading Teacher: Distinguished Educator Series, 49*(3), 182-190. Downloaded from http://globalconversationsinliteracy.files.wordpress.com/2011/08/cambourne-towardsedrelevanttheorylitlearning.pdf

49. Cambourne, B. (1988). *The Whole Story: Natural Learning and the Acquisition of Literacy in the Classroom*. New York, NY: Scholastic.

50. Harford, T. (2014, March 28). Big data: are we making a big mistake? *The Financial Times Magazine*. Retrieved from http://www.ft.com/cms/s/2/21a6e7d8-b479-11e3-a09a-00144feabdc0.html#axzz32t965jr3

51. Gates, B. (2009, July 21). *National Conference of State Legislatures (NCSL)*. Prepared remarks retrieved from http://www.gatesfoundation.org/media-center/speeches/2009/07/bill-gates-national-conference-of-state-legislatures-ncsl Note: The actual video presentation is different in places from these prepared remarks.

52. Gates, B. (2009, July 21). *National Conference of State Legislatures (NCSL)* Video excerpt retrieved from https://www.youtube.com/watch?v=xtTK_6VKpf4 Note: This actual video presentation is different in places from the prepared remarks.

53. "There is only power and those too weak to seek it." From Rowling, J.K. (1998). *Harry Potter and the Sorcerer's Stone.*

54. Rowling, J.K. (1998). *Harry Potter and the Sorcerer's Stone.* New York, NY: Scholastic.

55. "Come, the niceties will be observed." From Rowling, J.K. (2000). *Harry Potter and the Goblet of Fire.*

56. Rowling, J.K. (2000). *Harry Potter and the Goblet of Fire.* New York, NY: Scholastic.

57. U.S. Department of Education (2012, October 9). *Education Datapalooza: Unleashing the Power of Open Data to Help Students, Parents, and Teachers.* Retrieved from http://www.ed.gov/blog/2013/01/education-datapalooza-unleashing-the-power-of-open-data-to-help-students-parents-and-teachers/

58. Ferreira, J. (2012, October 9). Presentation at the U.S. Department of Education *Education Datapalooza: Unleashing the Power of Open Data to Help Students, Parents, and Teachers.* Retrieved from https://www.youtube.com/playlist?list=PLhdwy3ASoEfm1QeH0kfNnLWUqv4lE1pPs *or* https://www.youtube.com/watch?v=Lr7Z7ysDluQ&list=PLhdwy3ASoEfm1QeH0kfNnLWUqv4lE1pPs&index=19

59. Chomsky, N. (2014, February 14). *Chomsky on Academic Labor: How Higher Education Ought to Be.* Edited transcript of remarks given by Noam Chomsky via Skype on 4 February 2014 to a gathering of members and allies of the Adjunct Faculty Association of the United Steelworkers in Pittsburgh, PA. Transcript retrieved from http://www.towardfreedom.com/35-archives/labor/3460-chomsky-on-academic-labor-how-higher-education-ought-to-be

60. Gilens, M. and Page, B.I. (2014, April 9). Testing Theories of American Politics: Elites, Interest Groups, and Average Citizens. Forthcoming (2014, Fall). *Perspectives in Politics.* Downloaded from http://www.princeton.edu/~mgilens/Gilens-homepage-materials/Gilens-and-Page/Gilens-and-Page-202014-Testing-Theories-03-7-14.pdf

61. Cassidy, J. (2014, April 18). Is America An Oligarchy? *The New Yorker.* Retrieved from http://www.newyorker.com/online/blogs/johncassidy/2014/04/is-america-an-oligarchy.html

62. Winship, M., and Moyers, B. (2014, April 22). The 1% in America Are Turning into a Ruling Oligarchy at an Astonishing Pace. *AlterNet.* Retrieved from http://www.alternet.org/economy/1-america-are-turning-ruling-oligarchy-astonishing-pace

63. Bradatan, C. (2014, March 18). Herta Müller's Language of Resistance. *Boston Review.* Downloaded from https://www.bostonreview.net/books-ideas/costica-bradatan-herta-muller-cristina-double

64. Müller, H. (2013). *Cristina and Her Double: Selected Essays.* London, UK: Portobello Books.

65. Wilby, P. (2011, June 13). Mad professor goes global. *The Guardian.* Retrieved from http://www.theguardian.com/education/2011/jun/14/michael-barber-education-guru/print

66. Paxman, J., and Gates, B. (2014, January 23). *Jeremy Paxman interviews Bill Gates at Davos 2014*. Retrieved from https://www.youtube.com/watch?v=oq0u986edt0

67. Piketty, T. (2014). *Capital in the Twenty-First Century*. Cambridge, MA: Harvard University Press.

68. Piketty, T. (2014, April 16). *Capital in the Twenty-First Century*. Presentation at the City University of New York. Retrieved from https://www.youtube.com/watch?v=heOVJM2JZxI

69. The World's Billionaires. *Forbes*. Interactive listing updated daily. As retrieved on June 2, 2014, 1640 listed individuals with wealth ranging from #1640 at $748 million to #1 Bill Gates at $78 billion, total wealth $6.6 trillion. Retrieved from http://www.forbes.com/billionaires/list/37/#tab:overall

70. Giles, C. and Giugliano, F. (2014, May 23). Thomas Piketty's exhaustive inequality data turn out to be flawed. *Financial Times*. Retrieved from http://www.ft.com/intl/cms/s/0/c9ce1a54-e281-11e3-89fd-00144feabdc0.html?siteedition=intl#axzz33bvuvh4k

71. See also Taibbi, M. (2014). *The Divide: American Injustice in the Age of the Wealth Gap*. New York, NY: Spiegel & Grau.

72. Shin, L. (2014, January 23). The 85 Richest People In The World Have As Much Wealth As The 3.5 Billion Poorest. *Forbes*. Retrieved from http://www.forbes.com/sites/laurashin/2014/01/23/the-85-richest-people-in-the-world-have-as-much-wealth-as-the-3-5-billion-poorest/

73. Fuentes-Neva, R., and Galasso, N. (2014, January 20). Working for the Few: Political capture and economic inequality. *Oxfam International*. Summary and full reports retrieved from http://www.oxfam.org/en/policy/working-for-the-few-economic-inequality

74. Olmstead, K. (2014). *21st Century Family Literacy*, Doctoral dissertation, Hofstra University.

75. Gates, B. (2013, September 21). Question and answer session with David Rubenstein and Bill Gates at the Sanders Theater, Harvard University, at the launch of *The Harvard Campaign*. Video retrieved from http://alumni.harvard.edu/stories/harvard-campaign-launches *or* https://www.youtube.com/watch?v=cBHJ-8Bch4E

76. Murdoch, R. (2012, April 25). Evidence given by Rupert Murdoch before the Leveson inquiry. Video retrieved from http://www.theguardian.com/media/video/2012/apr/25/rupert-murdoch-leveson-inquiry-video

77. U.K. Parliament Culture, Media and Sport Select Committee. (2011, July 19). Oral Evidence by Rupert & James Murdoch. Video downloaded from http://www.theguardian.com/media/interactive/2011/jul/19/rupert-murdoch-hearing-interactive-presentation

78. U.K. Parliament Culture, Media and Sport Select Committee. (2011, July 19). Oral Evidence by Rupert & James Murdoch. Transcript of hearing downloaded from http://www.theguardian.com/news/datablog/2011/jul/20/james-rupert-murdoch-full-transcript

79. New York State Assembly Standing Committee on Education Public Hearing. (2014, February 28). *Disclosure of Personally Identifiable Student Information by School Districts and The State Education Department*. Video retrieved from http://nystateassembly.granicus.com/MediaPlayer.php?view_id=2&clip_id=936

80. New York State Assembly Standing Committee on Education Public Hearing. (2014, February 28). *Disclosure of Personally Identifiable Student Information by School Districts and The State Education Department*. Transcript of hearing retrieved from http://nystateassembly.granicus.com/DocumentViewer.php?file=nystateassembly_8903abcf9e8183c0c54c9b489d9a3f80.pdf&view=1

81. New York State Assembly Standing Committee on Education Public Hearing. (2013, November 20, 2013). *Disclosure of Personally Identifiable Student Information by School Districts and The State Education Department*. Video retrieved from http://nystateassembly.granicus.com/MediaPlayer.php?view_id=2&clip_id=769

82. New York State Assembly Standing Committee on Education Public Hearing. (2013, November 20, 2013). *Disclosure of Personally Identifiable Student Information by School Districts and The State Education Department*. Transcript of hearing retrieved from http://nystateassembly.granicus.com/DocumentViewer.php?file=nystateassembly_e2c03eb58ba905dea07fda8a4613cd09.pdf&view=1

83. House of Commons, Culture, Media and Sport Committee, Eleventh Report of Session 2010-2012, Volume 1 (2012, May 1). *News International and Phone-hacking*. Retrieved from http://www.publications.parliament.uk/pa/cm201012/cmselect/cmcumeds/903/90302.htm

84. Chomsky, N., Herman, E., and Lewis, J. (2011, September 21). The Myth of the Liberal Media: The Propaganda Model of News. *Media Education Foundation*. Video downloaded from https://www.youtube.com/watch?v=E8oHl3ooeZo

85. Chomsky, N., Herman, E., and Lewis, J. (2011, September 21). The Myth of the Liberal Media: The Propaganda Model of News. *Media Education Foundation*. Transcript of video downloaded from http://www.mediaed.org/assets/products/114/transcript_114.pdf

86. Barber, M., Day, S. et al (2014, March 24). The New Opportunity to Lead: A vision for education in Massachusetts in the next 20 years. *Massachusetts Business Alliance for Education*. Downloaded from http://www.mbae.org/wp-content/uploads/2014/03/New-Opportunity-to-Lead.pdf or http://www.mbae.org/new-report-offers-a-vision-for-education-in-the-next-20-years/

87. Vaznis, J. (2014, March 24). Mass. Schools require dramatic change, report says. *The Boston Globe*. Retrieved from http://www.bostonglobe.com/metro/2014/03/23/mass-schools-require-quick-dramatic-change-report-says/TBTiAvjnvkk38Jk2tHch1K/story.html

88. Barber, M. (2012, December 5). *Oceans of Innovation: Bring on the whole system education revolution!* Presentation by Michael Barber at the National Endowment for Science, Technology and Arts (Nesta), London, UK. Video downloaded from http://www.pearson.com/michael-barber/videos.html

89. Asimov, I. (1941). *Nightfall*. Retrieved from: http://www.uni.edu/morgans/astro/course/nightfall.pdf http://www.astro.sunysb.edu/fwalter/AST389/TEXTS/Nightfall.htm

90. Calvino, I. (1968). *The Daughters of the Moon*. In *The Complete Cosmicomics*. UK: Penguin Classics (2009). Also published in The New Yorker. (2009, February 23). Retrieved from http://www.newyorker.com/fiction/features/2009/02/23/090223fi_fiction_calvino

91. Bremmer, I. (2012). *Every Nation For Itself: Winners and Losers in a G-Zero world*.

New York, NY: Portfolio/Penguin.

92. Barber, M., Donnelly, K., and Rizvi, S. (2012, August). Oceans of Innovation: The Atlantic, the Pacific, global leadership and the future of education. *Institute for Public Policy Research*. Downloaded from http://www.ippr.org/assets/media/images/media/files/publication/2012/09/oceans-of-innovation_Aug2012_9543.pdf *or* http://www.ippr.org/publications/oceans-of-innovation-the-atlantic-the-pacific-global-leadership-and-the-future-of-education

93. Dobbs R., et al. (2012) *Urban world: Cities and the rise of the consuming class.* McKinsey Global Institute, Chicago: McKinsey and Company. Downloaded from http://www.mckinsey.com/insights/urbanization/urban_world_cities_and_the_rise_of_the_consuming_class

94. "It's mad," I say. "It's bad. And, it's brilliant." Adapted from Wintour, P. (2013, October 11). Dominic Cummings: genius or menace? *The Guardian*.

95. Wintour, P. (2013, October 11). Dominic Cummings: genius or menace? *The Guardian*. Retrieved from http://www.theguardian.com/politics/2013/oct/11/dominic-cummings-genius-menace-michael-gove/print

96. "...somehow they have lost their individuality and merged into a continuous shadowy mass." Adapted from Asimov, I. (1941). *Nightfall*.

97. Barber, M. (2012, August 13). Interview of Michael Barber by Sarah Montague on *BBC Hardtalk*. Full video (24 minutes) not available from BBC, video excerpt (5 minutes 27 seconds) downloaded from http://news.bbc.co.uk/2/hi/programmes/hardtalk/9744455.stm Full audio (24 minutes) downloaded from http://www.bbc.co.uk/podcasts/series/ht/all or http://downloads.bbc.co.uk/podcasts/worldservice/ht/ht_20120813-0100c.mp3

98. Diane Ravitch: http://dianeravitch.net/

99. Chomsky, N. (2011, April 7). *The State-Corporate Complex: A Threat to Freedom and Survival*. Presentation by Noam Chomsky, the Hart House Debates Committee, Near East Cultural and Educational Foundation (NECEF), and Science for Peace. Video downloaded from https://www.youtube.com/watch?v=MiGNB1VpdBY

100. Chomsky, N. (2011, April 7). *The State-Corporate Complex: A Threat to Freedom and Survival*. Presentation by Noam Chomsky, the Hart House Debates Committee, Near East Cultural and Educational Foundation (NECEF), and Science for Peace. Transcript downloaded from http://www.chomsky.info/talks/20110407.htm

101. Louis, C.K. (2014, April 28). My kids used to love math. Now it makes them cry. Thanks standardized testing and common core! *Twitter*. Downloaded from https://twitter.com/louisck/status/460765469746929664

102. Stephen Krashen: http://www.schoolsmatter.info/ *and* http://skrashen.blogspot.com/

103. Mark Garrison: http://www.markgarrison.net/

104. Morna McDermott: http://unitedoptout.com/about/

105. Anthony Cody: http://blogs.edweek.org/teachers/living-in-dialogue/

106. "...as the last thread of sunlight shining through the window thins out and snaps." Adapted from Asimov, I. (1941). *Nightfall*.

107. "There is a strange silence outside." Adapted from Asimov, I. (1941). *Nightfall*.

108. "For this is the Dark – the Dark and the Cold and the Doom. The bright walls of the universe are shattering and their awful Black fragments are falling …" Adapted from Asimov, I. (1941). *Nightfall*.

109. *Rule Britannia*. Lyrics by James Thomson (1763), music by Thomas Arne (1740). Video downloaded from https://www.youtube.com/watch?v=rB5Nbp_gmgQ (2009) https://www.youtube.com/watch?v=yprh8ElXgbU (2012) https://www.youtube.com/watch?v=AESZszvre3c&index=15&list=PL90FC40B3EA761E2F (2011) http://upload.wikimedia.org/wikipedia/commons/3/35/Rule%2C_Britannia.ogg (1914)

110. "Ah, music! ….A magic beyond all we do here!" From Rowling, J.K. (1998). *Harry Potter and the Sorcerer's Stone*.

111. Rowling, J.K. (1998). *Harry Potter and the Sorcerer's Stone*. New York, NY: Scholastic.

112. Murdoch, I. (1970). (2nd edition, 2001). *The Sovereignty of Good*. London, UK: Routledge.

113. Weil, S. (1952). (Classic edition, 2002). *Gravity and Grace*. London, UK: Routledge.

114. Susan Ohanian: http://www.susanohanian.org/

115. Diane Ravitch: http://dianeravitch.net/

116. Duncan, A. (2014, April 9). Speech at the *National Action Network* conference in New York City by U.S. Secretary of Education Arne Duncan. Quoted excerpt from speech retrieved from: http://ny.chalkbeat.org/2014/04/10/arne-duncan-urges-new-yorkers-to-stick-with-cuomo-on-teacher-evals/#.U4alaijDXio

117. Duncan, A. (2014, April 10). Speech at *New York University*. Video retrieved from http://vimeo.com/91657474

118. "Of course it is happening….It's happening inside your head. Why on earth should that mean that it is not real?" Adapted from Rowling, J.K. (2007). *Harry Potter and the Deathly Hallows*.

119. Rowling, J.K. (2007). *Harry Potter and the Deathly Hallows*. New York, NY: Scholastic.

120. Pickett, K.E. and Wilkinson, R. (2011). *The Spirit Level Age: Why Greater Equality Makes Societies Stronger*. London: Bloomsbury Publishing.

121. The Equality Trust: Because More Equal Societies Work Better For Everyone. *Resources: The Spirit Level*. Retrieved from http://www.equalitytrust.org.uk/resources/spirit-level

122. Calamia, M. (2013, October 20). Common Core Can Emotionally Damage Your Child! *The Independent Sentinel*. Retrieved from http://www.independentsentinel.com/common-core-can-emotionally-damage-your-child/ or http://stopccssinnys.com/uploads/Mary_Calamia_CCSS_Press_release.pdf

123. Calamia, M. (2013, October 10). Statement for the New York State Assembly Forum, Brentwood, New York. Text of prepared testimony retrieved from http://stopccssinnys.com/uploads/Al_Graf_-_Mary_Calamia_full_text.pdf

124. Calamia, M. (2013, October 20). Oral testimony at the New York State Assembly Forum, Brentwood, New York. Video retrieved from http://stopccssinnys.

com/AlGrafForums.html

125. *Rule Britannia*. Lyrics by James Thomson (1763), music by Thomas Arne (1740). Video downloaded from https://www.youtube.com/watch?v=rB5Nbp_gmgQ (2009) https://www.youtube.com/watch?v=yprh8ElXgbU (2012) https://www.youtube.com/watch?v=AESZszvre3c&index=15&list=PL90FC40B3EA761E2F (2011) http://upload.wikimedia.org/wikipedia/commons/3/35/Rule%2C_Britannia.ogg (1914)

126. Ohanian, S. (2013). Gates of Hell: Abandon all Hope, Ye Who Enter Here. In J. A. Gorlewski and B. J. Porfilio, (Editors), *Left Behind in the Race to the Top: Realities of School Reform*. Charlotte, NC: Information Age Publishing.

127. Heilemann, J. (2001). *Pride Before the Fall: The Trials of Bill Gates and the End of the Microsoft Era*. New York, NY: Harper Collins.

128. Ford, G. (2011 May 29). The Corporate Dream: Teachers as Temps. *Common Dreams*. Retrieved from https://www.commondreams.org/view/2011/05/29-2

129. Kennedy, D. (1995, December 29 – 1996, January 4). Bill Gates fights to keep the world safe for Microsoft. *Reviews*. Retrieved from http://bostonphoenix.com/alt1/archive/books/reviews/12-95/BILL_GATES.html

130. "When the hurly-burly's done, When the battle's lost and won. That will be'ere the set of sun." "Fair is foul and foul is fair, Hover through the fog and filthy air." From Shakespeare, W. *Macbeth*. Witches, Act I, Scene I.

131. Coleman, D. (2013, May 17). *Our Path to Ensuring College Success and Opportunity for All*. Presentation by David Coleman at the Strategic Data Project (SDP) Beyond the Numbers Convening, Boston, MA, May 15-17, 2013, From *Classroom to Boardroom: Analytics for Strategy and Performance*. Video downloaded from https://www.youtube.com/watch?v=IPoUmSfTTNI

132. Benn, T. (2006, November 15). *The Inaugural Benn Lecture*, Bristol, UK. Video downloaded from https://www.youtube.com/watch?v=x4wXi0zwP1M

133. Green, J. (2014, March 30). *Dear Mr. Gove*. A poem written and performed by Jess Green. Video downloaded from https://www.youtube.com/watch?v=qJ8RA3QF0EU&feature=kp

134. Cummings, D. (Undated). *Some thoughts on education and political priorities*. Undated paper (237 pages) referenced in *The Guardian* (Wintour, P., October 11, 2013), and downloaded from http://www.theguardian.com/politics/interactive/2013/oct/11/dominic-cummings-michael-gove-thoughts-education-pdf *or* http://static.guim.co.uk/ni/1381763590219/-Some-thoughts-on-education.pdf

135. Wintour, P. (2013, October 11). Genetics outweighs teaching, Gove advisor tells his boss. *The Guardian*. Retrieved from http://www.theguardian.com/politics/2013/oct/11/genetics-teaching-gove-adviser

136. Wilson, E.O. (1998). *Consilience: The Unity of Knowledge*. New York, NY: Alfred A Knopf.

137. Fodor, J. (1998, October 29). Look! Review of Consilience: The Unity of Knowledge by Edward O. Wilson. *London Review of Books, 20*(1), 3-6. Retrieved from http://www.lrb.co.uk/v20/n21/jerry-fodor/look

138. "It's mad," I say. "It's bad. And, it's brilliant." Adapted from Wintour, P. (2013,

October 11). Dominic Cummings: genius or menace? *The Guardian.*

139. Wintour, P. (2013, October 11). Dominic Cummings: genius or menace? *The Guardian.* Retrieved from http://www.theguardian.com/politics/2013/oct/11/dominic-cummings-genius-menace-michael-gove/print

140. *For He Is An Englishman,* from the Gilbert & Sullivan opera *HMS Pinafore.* Video downloaded from https://www.youtube.com/watch?v=u6_vyGuhkfA

141. Bennett, A. (2004). *The History Boys.* London, UK: Faber & Faber.

142. Bourdieu, P. (1999). *Acts of Resistance: Against the Tyranny of the Market.* New York, NY: The New Press.

143. Cleese, J., Barker, R., and Corbett, R. (1966). From the BBC's *The Class Collection: The Class Sketch,* with John Cleese, Ronnie Barker and Ronnie Corbett. Video downloaded from http://www.bbc.co.uk/comedy/collections/p00gs4vy#p00hhrwl

144. Cusick, J. (2013, February 15). 'Dump f***ing everyone': the inside story of how Michael Gove's vicious attack dogs are terrorizing the DfE. *The Independent.* Retrieved from http://www.independent.co.uk/news/education/education-news/dump-fing-everyone-the-inside-story-of-how-michael-goves-vicious-attack-dogs-are-terrorising-the-dfe-8497626.html

145. Edwards, A. (2013, October 12). 'Genetics outweighs teaching': Michael Gove's right hand man says it is IQ, not education, which determines child's future. *Mail Online.* Retrieved from http://www.dailymail.co.uk/news/article-2455623/Michael-Gove-advisor-Dominic-Cummings-claims-Genetics-outweighs-teaching.html

146. Sokal, A. D. (1996, Spring/Summer). Transgressing the Boundaries: Towards a Transformative Hermeneutics of Quantum Gravity. *Social Text,* 46/47, 217-252. Retrieved from http://www.physics.nyu.edu/sokal/transgress_v2/transgress_v2_singlefile.html

147. Sokal, A. D. (1996, May/June). A Physicist Experiments with Cultural studies. *Lingua Franca.* Retrieved from http://linguafranca.mirror.theinfo.org/9605/sokal.html

148. Gould, S. J. (1982). *The Mismeasure of Man.* New York, NY: W.W. Norton & Company.

149. Fortun, M., and Mendelsohn, E. (Editors). (1998). *The Practices of Human Genetics (Sociology of the Sciences Yearbook).* Dordrecht, The Netherlands: Kluwer Academic Publishers.

150. U.S. Department of Education, Office of Educational Technology (2013, February). *Promoting Grit, Tenacity, and Perseverance: Critical Factors for Success in the 21st Century.* (Pages 41-45). Retrieved from http://www.ed.gov/edblogs/technology/files/2013/02/OET-Draft-Grit-Report-2-17-13.pdf

151. *Council for International Organizations of Medical Sciences (CIOMS)* in collaboration with the *World Health Organization (WHO).* (2002). *International Ethical Guidelines for Biomedical Research Involving Human Subjects.* Retrieved from http://www.cioms.ch/publications/layout_guide2002.pdf

152. *Council for International Organizations of Medical Sciences (CIOMS):* http://www.cioms.ch/

153. Milgram, S. (1973, December). The perils of obedience. *Harper's Magazine.* Retrieved from http://harpers.org/archive/1973/12/the-perils-of-obedience/

154. Rich, A. (1979). *On Lies, Secrets, and Silence: Selected Prose 1966 – 1978*. New York, NY: W.W. Norton.

155. Woolf, V. (1938). *Three Guineas*. San Diego, CA: Harcourt.

156. Council on Foreign Relations (March, 2102). *Task Force Report No. 68: U.S. Education Reform and National Security*. Retrieved from http://www.cfr.org/united-states/uzsz-education-reform-national-security/p27618

157. Ibsen, H. (1879). (1992 Dover edition). *A Doll's House*. Mineola, NY: Dover.

158. Morna McDermott: http://unitedoptout.com/about/

159. Leonie Haimson, *Class Size Matters*: http://www.classsizematters.org/

160. Cody, A. (2014, forthcoming). *The Educator And The Oligarch*. New York, NY: Garn Press

161. Rich, A. (1972). *Toward a Woman-Centered University*. In *On Lies, Secrets, and Silence*: Selected Prose 1966 – 1978. New York, NY: W.W. Norton.

162. Arendt, H. (1958). *The Human Condition*, Chicago, IL: University of Chicago Press (2nd edition, 1998).

163. Morrison, T. (1992). *Jazz*. New York, NY: Alfred A Knopf.

164. Morrison, T. (1987). *Beloved*. New York, NY: Alfred A Knopf.

165. Morrison, T. (1993, December 7). *Nobel Lecture*. The Nobel Prize in Literature 1993. Retrieved from http://www.nobelprize.org/nobel_prizes/literature/laureates/1993/morrison-lecture.html

166. Woolf, V. (1929). *A Room of One's Own*. San Diego, CA: Harcourt, Brace and Company.

167. Shaughnessy, M.P. (1977). *Errors and Expectations: A Guide for the Teacher of Basic Writing*. New York, NY: Oxford University Press USA.

168. Rich, A. (1972). *When We Dead Awaken: Writing as Re-Vision*. In *On Lies, Secrets, and Silence: Selected Prose 1966 – 1978*. New York, NY: W.W. Norton.

169. Rich, A. (1972). *Anne Sexton: 1928 - 1974*. In *On Lies, Secrets, and Silence: Selected Prose 1966 – 1978*. New York, NY: W.W. Norton.

170. Sexton, A. (1964, July 14). *Little Girl, My String Bean, My Lovely Woman*. In Sexton, A. (1988). *Selected Poems of Anne Sexton*. Boston, MA: Houghton Mifflin Harcourt.

171. Greene, M. (1984, Fall). How Do We Think about Our Craft? *Teachers College Record, 86*(1), 55-67. Retrieved from https://maxinegreene.org/uploads/library/how_we_think_craft.pdf

172. Goodman, Y., Greene, M., Meek Spencer, M., and Rosenblatt, L. *Language, Literacy, Policies and Public Education*. International Scholars' Forum, Hofstra University, September 21, 2001.

173. Rosenblatt, L. (1938). *Literature as Exploration*. New York, NY: The Modern Language Association of America (1995, 5th edition).

174. Rosenblatt, L. (2001, October). Personal email communication.

175. Goodman, Y., Greene, M., Meek Spencer, M., and Rosenblatt, L. *Language,*

Literacy, Policies and Public Education. International Scholars' Forum, Hofstra University, September 21, 2001.

176. Morrison, T. (1970). *The Bluest Eye.* New York, NY: Alfred A. Knopf (2000).

177. Kropotkin, H. P. (1902). *Mutual Aid: A Factor of Evolution.* New York, NY: New York University Press (1972).

178. Maathai, W. (2004, December 10). *Nobel Lecture.* The Nobel Prize Peace Prize 2004. http://www.nobelprize.org/nobel_prizes/peace/laureates/2004/maathai-lecture-text.html

179. Goodman, Y, Reyes, I, and McArthur, K. (2005, March). Emilia Ferreiro: Searching for Children's Understandings about Literacy as a Cultural Object. *Language Arts, 82*(4), 318-323. Retrieved from http://www.ncte.org/journals/la/issues/v82-4 *or* http://eric.ed.gov/?id=EJ717539

180. Ferreiro, E. (2003). *Past and Present of the Verbs to Read and to Write.* Toronto, Ontario: Groundwood Books/Douglas & McIntyre.

181. Goodman, Y., Greene, M., Meek Spencer, M., and Rosenblatt, L. *Language, Literacy, Policies and Public Education.* International Scholars' Forum, Hofstra University, September 21, 2001.

182. Goodman, Y. (2014, February 9). Email communication.

183. Goodman, Y. Email communication.

184. Louis, C.K. (2014, April 28). My kids used to love math. Now it makes them cry. Thanks standardized testing and common core! *Twitter.* Downloaded from https://twitter.com/louisck/status/460765469746929664

185. Ravitch, D. (2014, May 2). *My Reply to Alexander Nazaryan of Newsweek.* Retrieved from http://dianeravitch.net/2014/05/02/my-reply-to-alexander-nazaryan-of-newsweek/

186. *Chariots of Fire* (1981). Historical drama movie about two British athletes at the 1924 Olympic Games.

187. " – but still, like dust, our spirits rise," adapted from the poem *Still I Rise* in Angelou, M. (1995). *Phenomenal Woman: Four Poems Celebrating Women.*

188. "Let us *not* praise famous men." Adapted from the title of Agee, J. (1939). *Let Us Now Praise Famous Men.*

189. Agee, J. (1939). *Let Us Now Praise Famous Men.* Boston, MA: Houghton Mifflin Harcourt (2000).

190. Rich, A. (1972). *Toward a Woman-Centered University.* In *On Lies, Secrets, and Silence: Selected Prose 1966 – 1978.* New York, NY: W.W. Norton.

Resistance to the Corporate Education Revolution

National Organizations and Resources

At The Chalk Face

Badass Teacher Association

Children Are More than Test Scores

Citizens United for Responsible Education (CURE)

Class Size Matters

Coalition for Public Education/Coalición por la EducaciónPública

Diane Ravitch

Education Liberty Watch

Educational Alchemy

Edutopia

Fair Test - The National Center for Fair and Open Testing

Fight Common Core (American Principles Project)

Going Public

Independent Community of Educators

Journey for Justice Alliance

Keep Education Local

Living in Dialogue

Lace To The Top - Students Are More Than A Test Score!

Mercedes Schneider

No Common Sense Education

Opportunity Action – Demanding Equity and Excellence in Education

Opt Out of State Standardized Tests

Parents Across America (PAA)

Parents And Educators Against Common Core Standards

Parents & Kids Against Standardized Testing

Rethinking Schools

Save Our Schools

Say No To Common Core

Stop Common Core – Reclaiming Local Control in Education

Susan Ohanian

The Answer Sheet (Valerie Strauss - Washington Post)

The Network For Public Education

Truth About Education – The Children's Voices

Truth in American Education

United Opt Out: The Movement to End Corporate Education Reform

Yong Zhao

National Organizations and Resources: Facebook Pages

At The Chalk Face

Badass Parents Association

Badass Parents Association (Group)

Badass Teacher Association

Badass Teacher Association (Group)

Choose To Refuse Common Core (Group)

Citizen Action for Fair Education (CAFE) (Group)

Citizens United for Responsible Education (CURE)

Class Size Matters

Common Core Critics (Group)

Common Core Critics – National Opt Out & Refuse the Test Campaign (Group)

Dump Duncan (Group)

Fair Test - The National Center for Fair and Open Testing

Fight Common Core (American Principles Project)

Going Public

Journey for Justice Alliance

Lace To The Top (Group)

Moms Against Duncan (MAD) (Group)

Opportunity Action – Demanding Equity and Excellence in Education

Opt Out of State Standardized Tests - National (Group)

Opt Out Of The State Test: The National Movement (United Opt Out) (Group)

National Opt Out & Refuse the Test Campaign

Parents Across America (PAA)

Parents and Educators Against Common Core Standards

Parents and Educators Against Common Core Standards (Group)

Parents and Teachers Against the Common Core (Group)

Rethinking Schools

Save Our Schools

Special Ed Advocates to Stop Common Core (Group)

Stop Common Core

Principals with Principles (Group)

Teachers' Letters to Obama (Group)

The Network For Public Education

Truth in American Education

United Opt Out National

State Organizations and Resources

Alabama - Stop Common Core in Alabama

Alaska - Stop the Common Core in Alaska

Arizona - Arizonans Against Common Core

Arkansas – Arkansas Against Common Core

California - Californians United Against Common Core

California – Parents for Public Schools (San Francisco)

Colorado – Denverites for Excellent Neighborhood School Education

Connecticut - Connecticut Coalition for Social Justice in Education Funding

Florida – Florida Parents Against Common Core

Florida – Floridians Against Common Core Education

Georgia - Stop Common Core in Georgia

Idaho - Idahoans for Local Education

Illinois- Parents United for Responsible Education (Chicago)

Illinois – Stop Common Core Illinois

Indiana – Hoosiers Against Common Core

Iowa - Iowans for Local Control

Kansas - Kansans Against Common Core

Kentucky - Kentuckians Against Common Core Standards

Maine - No Common Core Maine

Massachusetts - Can't Be Neutral

Michigan - Stop Common Core in Michigan

Minnesota - Minnesotans Against Common Core

Missouri – Missouri Coalition Against Common Core

Missouri – Missouri Education Watchdog

Nevada – Stop Common Core in Nevada

New Jersey - Education Law Center

New York - Abolish Common Core

New York – Allies for Public Education

New York - Campaign for Fiscal Equity

New York – Change The Stakes (NYC)

New York - Children should not be a number (NYS Stop Testing)

New York - Coalition for Public Education (NYC)

New York - Concerned Advocates for Public Education (NYC)

New York - Ed Notes Online (NYC)

New York – Education New York

New York - Grassroots Education Movement

New York - Independent Commission on Public Education (NYC)

New York – New York Collective of Radical Educators

New York – New York Principals

New York – No Common Sense Education

New York - NYC Educator

New York - NYC Public School Parents (NYC)

New York - NYS Allies For Public Education

New York - Parent Voices NY (NYC)

New York - Stop Common Core in New York State

New York - Stop Common Core in NY

New York – Teachers of Conscience (NYC)

New York - Teachers Unite (NYC)

New York - WNYers for Public Education

North Carolina – Durham Allies for Responsive Education (Durham)

Ohio - Ohioans Against Common Core

Oklahoma - Restore Oklahoma Public Education (ROPE)

Oregon – Oregon Save Our Schools

Oregon - Stop Common Core in Oregon

Pennsylvanian - Pennsylvanians Against Common Core

Pennsylvania – Parents United for Public Education (Philadelphia)

South Carolina – South Carolina Parents Involved in Education (SCPIE)

South Dakota - South Dakotans Against Common Core

Tennessee – Tennessee Against Common Core

Utah – Common Core: Education Without Representation

Utah - Utahns Against Common Core

Washington - Stop Common Core in Washington State

Wyoming – Wyoming Freedom in Education

Wyoming – Wyoming Against the Common Core

State Organizations and Resources: Facebook Pages

Alabama - Stop Common Core In Alabama

Alabama – Alabamians Against Common Core Standards in Education

Alaska - Alaskans Against the Common Core

Arizona - Mohave County Against Common Core (Group)

Arizona - Stop Common Core in Arizona (Group)

Arkansas - Arkansas Against Common Core (Group)

Arkansas - Arkansas Against Common Core

California - Californians Against Common Core (Group)

California - Stop Common Core in California

Colorado - Colorado Against Common Core

Colorado - Mesa County Citizens/Businesses Against Common Core Curriculum

Colorado - Parents and Educators Against Common Core Curriculum in Colorado

Colorado - Parent LED reform

Colorado - Stop Common Core in Colorado

Connecticut - Coalition for Social Justice in Education Funding

Connecticut - Stop Common Core In CT

Delaware - Delaware Against Common Core (Group)

Delaware - Delaware Against Common Core

Florida – Florida Common Core Watch

Florida - Stop Common Core in Florida

Florida – Central Florida Parents Against Common Core (FPACC) (Group)

Georgia - Stop Common Core In Georgia

Georgia - Georgians to Stop Common Core (Group)

Hawaii – Stop Common Core in Hawaii

Idaho - Idahoans Against Common Core

Idaho - Idahoans for Local Education

Idaho – Stop Common Core in Idaho

Illinois - Stop Common Core in Illinois

Indiana – Hoosiers Against Common Core

Indiana - Hoosier Moms Say No To Common Core

Iowa - Iowans for Local Control

Iowa – Stop Common Core in Iowa

Kansas - Kansans Against Common Core

Kentucky - Kentuckians Against Common Core Standards

Louisiana – Concerned Parents Against Common Core (Group)

Louisiana - Parents and Educators Against Common Core in Louisiana

Louisiana - Stop Common Core in Louisiana

Maine - No Common Core Maine

Maryland - Marylanders Against Common Core

Maryland - Stop Common Core in Maryland

Maryland - Stop Common Core in Maryland (Group)

Massachusetts - Can't Be Neutral

Michigan - Stop Common Core in Michigan

Minnesota – Minnesota Against Common Core

Mississippi - Stop Common Core In Mississippi

Missouri – Missouri for the Removal of Common Core

Missouri – Missouri Education Watchdog

Missouri – Missouri For Local Education (Group)

Montana – Montana Against Common Core (Group)

Montana - Stop Common Core in Montana

Nebraska - Nebraska Parents & Educators Against Common Core

Nevada - Nevadans Against Common Core (Group)

Nevada - Nevada Parents & Teachers STOP Common Core (Group)

Nevada - Nevada Parents & Teachers STOP Common Core

Nevada - Parent Led Reform Nevada - Stop Common Core (Group)

New Hampshire - School Choice for New Hampshire

New Hampshire - Stop Common Core in New Hampshire

New Hampshire - NH Families for Education (Group)

New Jersey - Cure NJ

New Jersey - Citizen Action for Fair Education (CAFE) (Group)

New Jersey - The Committee to Combat Common Core Curriculum (Group)

New Mexico - Stop Common Core In New Mexico

New York - Change The Stakes (NYC)

New York - Heads Down, Thumbs Up, Hudson Valley, N.Y.

New York - Long Island Opt-Out Info (Group)

New York - Long Island Parents and Teachers Against Standardized Testing & APPR

New York – Long Islanders United Against the Common Core

New York - NY Parents Opposed to Data Sharing without Consent! (Group)

New York – New York BATs (Group)

New York - Opt Out of State Standardized Tests (Group)

New York - Oswego County for Public Education Discussion Group (Group)

New York - Parents & Teachers Against Common Core (Group)

New York - Pencils DOWN Rockland County

New York - New York Grassroots Against Common Core (Group)

New York - NYS Refuse the Tests (Group)

New York - Rethinking Testing: Mid-Hudson Region

New York - STACCT: Southern Tier Against Common Core and Testing (Group)

New York - Staten Island - Know "Common Core" (Group)

New York - Stop Common Core in Cayuga/Onondaga County (Group)

New York - Stop Common Core in New York Catholic Schools (Group)

New York - Stop Common Core in New York -Monroe County (Group)

New York – Stop Common Core in NY

New York - Stop Common Core in New York State (Group)

New York - Stop Common Core in NYS Dutchess County (Group)

New York - Stop Common Core in Westchester County, NY (Group)

New York - Video Blast! Tell your New York State Common Core Story (Group)

North Carolina - Stop Common Core in NC

North Dakota - Stop Common Core in North Dakota

Ohio – Boardman Spartans Against Common Core (Group)

Ohio Educators and Parents Against Common Core Curriculum

Ohio - Ohio Common Core - Reality of Education Standards & Reform

Ohio – Ohio Parents and Teachers Against Common Core (Group)

Ohio - Stop Common Core in Ohio (Group)

Oklahoma – Oklahoma Parents and Educators for Public Education (Group)

Oklahoma - Restore Oklahoma Public Education (ROPE)

Oregon - Parent Led Reform - Oregon

Oregon - Stop Common Core in Oregon (Group)

Pennsylvanian - Pennsylvanians Against Common Core

Rhode Island - Stop Common Core in Rhode Island

Rhode Island - Rhode Islanders Against Common Core

South Carolina - Stop Common Core in South Carolina

South Dakota - South Dakotans Against Common Core

Tennessee - Stop Common Core in Tennessee

Tennessee – Education Matters Institute

Texas - Texans Against CSCOPE (Group)

Utah - Utahns Against Common Core

Virginia - Against Common Core in Virginia (Group)

Virginia - Eye on Virginia Education

Virginia - Stop Common Core in Virginia (Group)

Virginia - Virginians Concerned about K12 Education (Group)

Washington - Washington State Against Common Core State Standards (Group)

Washington - Washington State Against Common Core State Standards

West Virginia - West Virginia Against Common Core

Wisconsin - Stop Common Core in Wisconsin

Wyoming - Stop Common Core in Wyoming (Group)

Other Organizations and Resources

American Principles Project - Education

Cato Institute - Common Core: The Great Debate

Common Core - Education Without Representation

Common Core Issues

Common Core Issues - Video Website

Common Core Movie Trailer for "Building the Machine"

Common Crud Scans/Photos of Common Core Curriculum Assignments) (Group)

Common Dreams

Inappropriate Common Core Lessons (Group)

Only a Teacher (PBS Series)

Stop the National Common Core Power Grab: Reclaim Local Control of Education Video

The Educational Freedom Coalition (Educational Provider Data Base/ Alignment with CCSS)

Truth in American Education (Audio/Video Resources)

Truthout

CLIMATE CHANGE: ORGANIZATIONS AND RESOURCES

Convention on Biodiversity (CBD)

Diversitas

Future Earth

Global Carbon Project (GCP)

Intergovernmental Panel on Climate Change (IPCC)

Intergovernmental Platform on Biodiversity & Ecosystem Services (IPBES)

International Council for Science (ICSU)

International Geosphere-Biosphere Programme (IGBP)

International Human Dimensions Programme on Global Environmental Change (IHDP)

International Social Science Council (ISSC)

National Aeronautics and Space Administration (NASA)

National Oceanic and Atmospheric Administration (NOAA)

Nobel Cause Interdisciplinary Symposia

Planet Under Pressure 2012

Potsdam Institute for Climate Impact Research (PIK)

Stockholm Resilience Centre

The Royal Society

UK Met Office

United Nations Environmental Program (UNEP)

United Nations Framework Convention on Climate Change (UNFCCC)

United Nations System Work on Climate Change

US National Academy of Sciences

World Climate Research Programme (WCRP)

World Meteorological Organization (WMO)

ABOUT THE AUTHOR

Denny Taylor is Professor Emerita of Literacy Studies at Hofstra University, and the founder and CEO of Garn Press. She lives in a studio the size of a bookshelf in New York City. She writes every day and spends a lot of time trying not to buy any more books. Fortunately she is not very successful at not buying! Books are her greatest pleasure, and publishing them has become as exciting as writing them. She views the construction of eBooks as a craft as well as a technical feat.

Taylor is a lifelong activist and scholar committed to nurturing the imagination and human spirit, and she regards art, literature, and science as inseparable. She prefers actionable knowledge over right or left ideology, and she always wants to see the raw data rather than read the spin about it.

Taylor's doctoral dissertation was published in 1983 as *Family Literacy*, is still in print, and is regarded a classic within the field; *Growing Up Literate* received the Mina P. Shaughnessy award in 1988 from the Modern Language Association of America; and *Toxic Literacies* was nominated for both the Pulitzer Prize and the National Book Award. In 2004, Taylor was inducted into the *International Reading Association's Reading Hall of Fame*.

Most recently, Taylor's trans-disciplinary research has incorporated both the physical and social sciences. She participated in the June, 2010 International Science Council (ICSU) forum at UNESCO in Paris, which focused on developing a vision of new institutional frameworks for Global Sustainability Research (Earth System Visioning). She subsequently authored four peer reviewed research papers which combined data from the social and physical sciences that were presented at the *Planet Under Pressure* Conference in London in March, 2012.

Taylor brings all of her experience to Garn. Caring deeply about People and the Planet, about Language and Social Policy, and about Imagination and the Human Spirit, she has made these the three imprint pillars of Garn Press.

"We are making Garn the people's press," Taylor says. "Our mission is actionable knowledge, and we want to make Garn Press synonymous with social action."

Books by Denny Taylor

Forthcoming Garn Press Books by Denny Taylor

Keys To The Future: A Teacher's Guide To Making The Earth A Child Safe Zone

Rosie's Umbrella (a novel)

Educated or Indoctrinated?

Fukushima - Can Science Save Us? Can Policy Makers Can Pass The Car Battery Test?

Death of Childhood

People And The Planet: The Great Acceleration From Adaptation to Transformation

Other Books by Denny Taylor

Nineteen Clues: Great Transformations Can Be Achieved Through Collective Action (2014)

Beginning to Read and the Spin Doctors of Science (1998)

Many Families, Many Literacies: An International Declaration of Principles (1997)

Teaching and Advocacy (1997)

Toxic Literacies: Exposing the Injustice of Bureaucratic Texts (1996)

From The Child's Point Of View (1993)

Learning Denied: Inappropriate Educational Decision Making (1990)

Growing Up Literate, Learning From Inner City Families (1988)

Family Storybook Reading (1986)

Family Literacy: Young Children Learning to Read and Write (Second Edition, 1998)

Family Literacy: Young Children Learning to Read and Write (First Edition, 1983)

GARN PRESS

NEW YORK, NY

CPSIA information can be obtained at www.ICGtesting.com
Printed in the USA
BVOW03s1855011014

369136BV00004B/9/P